T5-ACY-012

FACE TO FACE

Shirley Faye

A KISMET™ Romance

METEOR PUBLISHING CORPORATION
Bensalem, Pennsylvania

KISMET™ is a trademark of Meteor Publishing Corporation

Copyright © 1990 Shirley T. Shiver
Cover Art copyright © 1990 Jack Martin

All rights reserved.

No part of this book may be reproduced, stored in a retrieval system, or transmitted in any form, by any means, including mechanical, electronic, photocopying, recording or otherwise, without prior written permission of the publisher, Meteor Publishing Corporation, 3369 Progress Drive, Bensalem, PA 19020.

First Printing October 1990.

ISBN: 1-878702-15-7

All the characters in this book are fictitious. Any resemblance to actual persons, living or dead, is purely coincidental.

Printed in the United States of America

This one's for Jim.
Thanks for the last 33 years.
What are you doing for the next 33? . . . and beyond?

SHIRLEY FAYE

Shirley is a native Floridian who stopped off in Texas on her way to Alaska 20 years ago. An avid reader, she discovered contemporary romance in the late 70's and has been hooked ever since. Her "real job" is Laboratory Technician for a Utility company. Shirley has been married 33 years (to the same man), has four children (who are grown and gone!), and her spare time is spent alternating between staring out the window and at a computer screen thinking "What if . . . ?"

PROLOGUE

"Hel-lo, darling." The curvaceous redhead almost drooled the words as she slid her hands up Damon Law's chest and clasped them behind his neck. "I didn't know you were in Texas. Hor-rible climate. But I just might be able to tolerate this outlandish heat," Lissa Andrews smiled up at the golden giant standing before her, "now that you're here!"

The cynical lines around Damon's mouth deepened and boredom settled around him, enveloping him like a cloak. The muscles of his well-developed shoulders rippled under the ragged folds of his faded T-shirt as he grasped her wrist in an iron grip.

As he pushed her out of his space, he watched the changing expressions on her face. They ran the gamut from seduction to disbelief, anger, and back to seduction in less than a second. His left eyebrow raised, giving a sardonic twist to his face.

"Oh, Damon!" Lissa smiled placatingly at him. "You're not still upset with me." Her forced laughter was a combination of anger at the man and a rueful admission to herself that she just might have screwed up royally this time.

"Upset? With you?" The hard smile on Damon's mouth did not reach his eyes. He pushed away from the wall and towered over her. Flicking her cheek with a careless finger, he drawled, "Now why would you think that?" His southern accent did not soften the harsh impact of his sarcasm.

The practiced smile on her perfectly made-up face slipped, and a glimmer of fear flashed in her eyes. "You're a cold, heartless, arrogant son of a bitch!" Lissa glared at her former lover. Hiding her seething emotions behind a brilliant smile, she continued. "Someday, Damon Law, you're going to fall in love. And I hope to hell I'm there to gloat when she kicks you in the teeth and tells you to get lost!"

With a sexy, hip-rolling walk, Lissa Andrews turned her back on Damon Law and rejoined the party.

ONE

Damon Law leaned against the side of the house and stared cynically at the crowd that was partying around the Olympic-size pool. He had been noticed, and a wave of awareness rolled toward him like the ever-widening circle on a smooth body of water.

Though he would never be comfortable being the cynosure of all eyes, he had come to terms with the fact that he drew attention wherever he went. The candid scrutiny had as much to do with his six-foot-five, two-hundred-twenty-pound body as with his position of power in the film industry.

Once he would have relished the attention. Now he didn't care that he was the focal point of these sated, bored, overindulged individuals' interest.

Damon shifted his broad shoulders against the side of the house. He would be the first to admit that *he* was as sated, bored, and overindulged as those he dismissed so casually. His years of success, with the attendant "yes men," hangers-on, and fawning women—all out for what they could get—had caused him to withdraw, to become an observer, apart from the crowd.

"Christi! Are you going to hide here all day?" Parker asked in an accusing voice. His irritation was tempered with both amusement and exasperation as he realized that Christiana had found the only isolated table on the patio.

"I might." Christiana shrugged.

"Christi, so help me—"

"Don't start, Parker. I was sitting here wondering why I let you bully me into coming to this bout of organized mayhem masquerading as a party," she interrupted before he began to lecture. "I don't particularly care for the music, I don't drink," she waved her lemonade cup in the air, "and I never learned how to flirt. I just don't fit in with this crowd. So why did you insist on my being here?"

"To get you out of that house you stay cooped up in, that's why," Parker Lloyd said bluntly.

"Why? I'm content."

"Dammit, Christi! You're not living—you're stagnating . . . barely existing. It's been a long time since the accident. I've pushed and prodded you this far. I'll be damned if I'll sit by and watch all my hard work go down the drain because you won't face reality. You've got to get out, meet people, have fun."

"Parker! Hey, buddy, come on! Where're you hiding?" a deep voice with a marked southern accent boomed over the noise of the party.

"Oh, hell." Parker glanced over his shoulder. "Stay here," he said sternly to Christiana. "I'll be right back."

Striding quickly, he intercepted the big, golden-haired man before he reached the table where Christi was sitting. He didn't want Damon Law anywhere near his guileless friend. He was too smooth, too sophisticated.

"Damon, you old son-of-a-gun! You made it!"

"Parker . . ." Damon's face split into a wide grin when he saw his lanky, red-haired, freckle-faced host. "Nice place you've got here."

"You know what they say," Parker laughed as he grasped Damon's hand in a strong grip. "It's humble, but it's home." He swept his arm in a wide arc, indicating the sprawling, lakeside mansion.

The disbelieving look on Damon's face spoke volumes. "You're the only man I know who would refer to a multimillion dollar home as 'humble!' Why didn't you warn me that Houston's traffic was as bad, if not worse, than L.A.'s?" he groused good-naturedly as he snagged a long-neck beer from a passing waiter.

"Hey. I didn't want to scare you away before you got here," Parker joked. "Besides, it's not that bad."

"Could have fooled me. I see you still know how to throw a spectacular party." He winced when the heavy-metal band broke into a loud, discordant melody. "If the local law doesn't pay us a visit, it will surprise me. Five'll get you ten that before the night's over, a neighbor complains about the music."

"Nah. I invited all the neighbors. I learned my lesson last summer in L.A. when we got run in for disturbing the peace."

"You mean the time you walked off with my date?"

"Oh." Parker was all innocence. "You mean she was with *you*?"

Damon shook his head, a wry smile indicating his resigned acceptance of Parker's antics. The man was incorrigible.

"Have you seen Lissa yet?" Parker asked. "I invited her just for you."

Damon grimaced. "Thanks a lot!"

"Uh oh. I take it from that face you pulled that she's history. Sorry."

"That's all right. You didn't know."

"My friend . . ." Parker slapped him on the back. "You need to circulate! There's plenty of food, booze, and beautiful people! One of the three ought to take your mind off your troubles!"

Parker watched Damon move into the crowd before he returned to Christi.

"Who was that?" Christiana asked Parker, her voice tinged with disgust.

"That overmuscled blond giant, Christi, is every woman's dream walking around on two feet."

"Dream?" Her soft "huh" of disgust was more damning than a whole stream of invectives. "He sounded more like a nightmare."

"Hold that thought. I want you to stay away from that one."

"Umm."

"Umm yourself. Don't think you are going to make me forget what we were discussing before we were interrupted. Christiana, I'm serious. It's time for you to broaden your horizons."

Stalling, Christiana ran her fingers around the rim of her cup until she reached the straw. Placing it in her lips, she pulled the cool lemonade into her mouth. An empty, sputtering sound echoed loudly in the silence that stretched between her and her best friend.

"But not with the blonde giant," she said finally.

"Yeah," Parker grinned at her mocking tone, "not with him."

"Oh, Parker. Make up your mind. You either want me to meet eligible men or you don't. Sometimes I wonder about you. Do you really want me to meet other men?" she asked, aiming a smile in his direction that took the sting out of her words.

"What the hell do you mean by that crack?" Parker's head snapped around and he stared at her.

"Think about it. You drag me to these affairs, then tell me—no, you order me—to stay away from every man I meet."

"Not every man," he said defensively, "just the womanizers."

"But, Parker . . ." she protested with a laugh, "the only kind of men you know are womanizers. So the question is, what do you want?"

He hitched his chair closer to her and spoke from behind his hand. "I'll tell ya, sweetheart," he teased in a bad Bogart imitation, "what I really want is you! But," he heaved a deep, theatrical sigh, "I know you look on me as a brother, and my mama didn't raise no fool for a son."

"Your mama didn't raise you, period. You were raised by a board of trustees bigger than all five of the major oil companies combined, remember?"

"Shh." His laughter held a touch of long hidden pain. "I'm trying to forget. Seriously, Christi," he continued, "Johnny's dead. You, whether you act like it or not, are alive. You've poked around that house by yourself for two years now, and it's time for you to get on with your life."

"I'm not by myself. I have Peggy and Billy Joe."

"A maid and a handyman. That's not what I meant, and you know it."

"I'm sorry, Parker. I'm not being obtuse deliberately, but I don't feel alone." She chewed on her lower lip. "How can I say this without sounding like a silly, lovestruck fool?" she asked with a little laugh. "I loved Johnny, and he loved me. I don't believe there can be another love like that for me. Not ever again," she choked. Clearing her throat she continued. "And truthfully, Parker, don't you think that after having known real love, I'd be a fool to settle for second best?"

At that moment the band broke into a particularly discordant tune. Clapping her hands over her ears, Christi stood. "How about walking me down to the creek? I've enjoyed about as much of this as I can stand."

"I can take you down there, but I can't stay with you," Parker grumbled. "Dammit! This isn't going like it was supposed to. I badgered you into coming to this party to mingle with other people. Maybe even meet another man. After what you just said, I doubt if there's another man on the face of the earth, much less in Houston, Texas, who stands a chance of getting near you, much less winning your love!"

"Well, hallelujah! You're finally getting the idea!"

Damon gave a self-derisive laugh and a philosophical shake of his head at the wicked grin the blonde flashed at him over her shoulder.

They had been enjoying a light flirtation when her date returned from water skiing, and she began trying to play them against each other. Not wanting to get involved in the lady's vicious game, Damon bowed out.

He grinned again as he watched her wiggle her rear enticingly as she walked away, clinging to her date's arm. The little tease was still at it.

He grabbed another long neck from a barrel of iced

beer as he pushed his way through the crowd, seeking a quieter, less crowded area. The steamy, East Texas sun beat down on his back, causing rivulets of sweat to run down his muscular body. The sticky sweat pooled in the hollow of his lower back before soaking into the waistband of his cut-offs. Pressing the ice-encrusted bottle to his cheek, he savored the shock of cold against his overheated flesh.

Overriding the heat, the laughter, and the noise of the heavy metal band, was a prickling sense of . . . what? He had the strongest sense of anticipation—like a kid on Christmas morning. He moved his shoulders in an unconscious, shrugging gesture. Nothing was going to happen here that hadn't happened at any one of hundreds of other parties he had attended.

Wandering aimlessly across the lawn, he avoided being sucked into groups of laughing, noisy people. Circling the house, he stumbled onto a path leading into the woods. Welcoming the cool shade and the privacy offered by the thick pines, he followed it.

His rambling thoughts settled again on the blonde and her games. What would it be like, he wondered, to find a woman who looked at him and saw a human being rather than a "personality" to be used?

He reached the end of the path and stepped up onto a redwood deck that jutted out over a small creek. Bracing his hands on the rail, he gazed moodily into the slow-moving water. He felt like he was staring down a long, empty tunnel that led to his future.

A tunnel containing nothing and going nowhere.

Christi shifted restlessly on the lounge. It was hot, and miserably muggy, even for the Houston area. Sitting up, she swept her dark glasses off and placed them on the deck under the lounge.

She twisted, fidgeting, trying to get comfortable. If Parker hadn't been so insistent, she would be home, in her own backyard. She certainly wouldn't be here, subjecting herself to the stares of all these strangers! Flopping over on her stomach, she stretched her feet out over the end of the cushion and wiggled her toes.

Damon stiffened at the sibilant sound made by bare skin sliding over cloth. He'd thought he was alone on the deck, but obviously he wasn't.

Hidden behind a screen of potted plants he saw a pair of legs, a woman's legs, resting on the striped cushion of a chaise longue. The feet attached to the sleek legs were delicately arched.

He leaned one elbow on the rail and studied what he could see of the long legs through the plants. Then a slight breeze pushed the fronds to one side, and he saw her clearly for a moment.

Automatically, he catalogued what he had seen. Tall, slender, with dark-brown hair hanging over her shoulder in a single long braid. Ordinary face, no makeup, no curves.

He resented her presence in his hideaway. Deliberately, he turned his back. Maybe if he ignored her, he'd get lucky and she'd go away.

Damon returned to staring at the creek, trying to regain his earlier, solitary apathy. It was no use. He was sharply aware of the woman on the lounge. He found himself straining his ears, listening for her next move. A moment later he was rewarded by the swishing sound of her slender legs moving on the cushion.

How did he know it was her legs?

He squeezed his eyes shut. It could have been an

arm sliding over the mat, graceful fingers caressing heavy cotton cloth. But it wasn't. He was positive it was her long, sexy legs. He could picture them, moving enticingly on the colorful, striped cotton. He stared at the creek, trying to force her out of his mind. Oh, hell! She was turning over again.

Slowly, fighting his reaction to this unknown flirt, he turned to watch her. He was torn between a desire to tell her to get lost, and an equally strong desire to take her up on her sensual invitation. A cynical twist to his lips was the only outward sign of the silent battle he fought.

"What the hell?" Giving up the fight, he swore softly as he sauntered over to her.

"Who's there?" Christi jerked around to face the intruder. Dammit. She didn't want company. She didn't want pity. And she had no desire to engage in meaningless chitchat. She'd come to this secluded spot to be alone.

"Hello." He spoke in a soft southern drawl. Christi felt the cushion of the lounge give as he sat beside her.

"Hello." Her greeting was abrupt as she recognized the soft southern voice. Her unwanted visitor was the man Parker had warned her to stay away from!

"I didn't see you up at the pool."

"No."

"Why not?"

"I don't swim."

"Neither do the other women up there. Most of them would probably melt if they got wet," he chuckled.

"Look, . . ." Christiana said, "no offense, but would you please go away?"

"Go away?"

"Yes. Like in disappear. Get lost. Vamoose." She

waved a slender hand in the air, gesturing toward the house and the loud, noisy party.

"Go away!" He was stunned. This woman had been flirting with him for the last half hour, giving him a silent but eloquent invitation. Now she was bluntly telling him to get lost! What kind of game was she playing? Dammit! He'd had his fill of women who flirted and promised, then drew back at the last minute. This one, at least, would not get away with it.

"No."

"No?" Now Christi was stunned—and a little apprehensive. "Why not?"

"Why? Because we've got some unfinished business to take care of, that's why."

"What unfinished business?"

"This."

Strong hands grasped her shoulders and gently pressed her down onto her back. A masculine scent of cologne, tobacco, beer, and a slight musky odor invaded her senses.

The sudden onset of a passionate kiss, combined with the weight of a heavy male body pushing her into the cushion took Christi's breath away. Shocked into immobility, she froze. Then instinct took over and she reached for the man who was expertly kissing her toward oblivion. It had been so long.

Johnny? she thought hazily, arching her neck to rub her cheek against the face of the man whose kiss was awakening her slumbering desires. *No. Not Johnny. Stranger.*

Not Johnny? What was she doing, kissing a stranger? Even worse, she was reacting passionately to his kiss. She began to push against the shoulders that pinned her to the cushion.

"What's this?" The southern drawl was thicker and slower. "Changing your mind?"

Damon pulled back and looked intently at the woman. Had he misread her invitation? He didn't think so.

"You stupid jackass! Get off me!" she spat furiously.

Okay, Law, so maybe you made a mistake. Maybe she wasn't flirting with you. Maybe all her sexy little movements weren't a come-on. He thought about her slow twists and turns, the tantalizing way her slim legs caressed the cushion.

The hell she wasn't!

But something happened that he hadn't planned. He *wanted* to kiss her again! Caught up in his own ploy, he captured her mouth with his. This time the kiss was soft and seductive. He teased. He nibbled. He nipped and licked.

And Christi's body betrayed her.

She felt his hair sliding through her fingers. Vaguely, she wondered when her hands had found their way from pushing against his massive shoulders to clutching his well-shaped head. He was so strong. So very male. She inhaled his scent and found it intoxicating.

Christi's hands shifted to his shoulders, her sensitive fingers learning the muscles that rippled under his smooth skin. His heavy weight against her breast felt so good. His fingers grazed her scalp as they threaded through her braid, loosening her hair. Each feather-light touch caused shivers to chase up and down her spine. She yielded to the expert technique of the experienced man who was kissing her so seductively.

Damon was drunk on the taste of her—addicted to the silk of her skin pressing against his body, awakening something rare and precious.

He wanted, he *needed*, her fiery response singing to his heated blood. He traced her mouth, alternately sucking her lower lip into the warm cavern of his mouth and touching her lips with delicate flicks of his tongue. He savored her taste like fine wine, dipping deep into her mouth to reach the sweetest, most tantalizing places.

Somewhere in the back of his mind a warning sounded. The kiss had escalated into something he had never intended. He was close to losing control.

The soft keening sounds that came from the back of Christi's throat registered fleetingly in her mind. She knew where this journey was taking her. She had been there before. But never, *never*, like this!

Christi moaned. *Please*. The word echoed in her head. Had she said it out loud? It didn't matter. The plea throbbed with every wild, runaway pulse beat that distributed the heat of desire throughout her body.

Damon groaned. He had to break it off! Now! Breathing heavily, he forced himself to pull away. His head was swimming, and his eyes wouldn't focus.

He looked from his shaking hands to the passion-flushed face of the slender woman. Her glazed eyes stared past his shoulder. From all appearances, she was as shaken as he.

Shook? Him? Over a *kiss*? Good God! What had happened here? The kiss had turned on him. What had started out as playful comeupance for a flirt had turned into an ambush. With sudden insight he knew that he had given a part of himself to this woman, a part that he would never get back.

He had to regain control!

"Be careful what you ask for in the future, sweetheart," he said thickly. "You just might get it."

Laughing ruefully at the whims of fate, Damon pushed himself away from the silent woman and stood on wobbly legs. With careful, painstaking movements, he walked unsteadily across the deck and back up the path toward the party.

"What?" With a start Christiana snapped out of the trancelike state induced by the passionate kiss. She tried to sit up but fell weakly back on the cushion. Her breathing was deep, ragged. What had happened to her?

She realized vaguely that she should be doing *something!* She should be outraged. She should be screaming her head off.

But all she could do was lie there and listen to his soft, mocking laughter receding in the distance. Even his laughter, she noticed, had a southern accent.

TWO

The heavy metal band was gone. Instead of hard rock, soft dinner music drifted on the evening air. While the guests changed from wet swimsuits to designer originals, other changes had taken place around the pool. Now the patio was dotted with intimate tables for two. Tiki lights, fueled with perfumed oil, lit the area while discouraging night-flying insects.

Christiana sat where Parker had left her—on the deck overlooking the patio. Wearing a pale-yellow sundress with spaghetti straps, she sat quietly, her hands folded in her lap. The fitted bodice flattered her soft curves, and the full skirt swirled around her long legs.

Her cool appearance presented an outward composure that was totally false. She was still shaken by her reaction to the stranger. Only her closest friend could have detected signs of her agitation, and he was busy being a genial host.

Christi's first thought after recovering from the passionate kiss had been to find Parker. She knew what he would do. For a brief, glorious moment, she'd relished the thought of the stranger lying in a bloody heap at her feet. But even as the picture formed in her mind, she'd known she wouldn't tell Parker.

Hadn't she sworn, when she left her parents' home in East Texas and returned to The Woodlands, to stand on her own two feet? Wasn't she determined to run her own life, without leaning on friends and family? Was she so weak, so spineless, that she would cry for help at the first sign of trouble?

No!

With a slight shake of her head and a self-conscious smile she returned to the present. The afternoon was over. Past. History. Then why was she still so agitated? Fear? Yes, she thought with her characteristic honesty, she was afraid. But of what? What was it that stretched her nerves and made her so tense?

Honesty forced her to admit that it was not being kissed by a stranger that bothered her. It was her uninhibited physical reaction to this unknown man that had her so upset.

Christi crossed her legs and settled more comfortably into her chair. She made a concerted effort to think about something, anything, else.

If only she could forget the scent of him. Even now, on the deck above the swimming pool, with all Parker's guests milling around below, she still thought she could smell that particular mingling of expensive scent and male musk that marked her sensual assailant.

Damon had changed out of the ragged cut-offs he'd worn earlier. Now he wore a pair of pale-blue Alexander Julian slacks with a soft cotton shirt of the same color. His eyes darted rapidly over the crowd on the patio below. Suddenly bored, he turned his back on the scene. His lean hips braced on the guard rail, he stared idly toward the house—and saw Christiana.

She was sitting quietly, her hands folded in her lap. Damon watched her cross her long legs and settle more comfortably into her chair.

God, he thought, *she's cool. She's just sitting there, looking straight through me as though I don't exist.*

His glance raked her from head to foot. Throughout his minute inspection, she sat still, making no attempt to attract him. He didn't quite know what to make of her. Model-thin, with her coronet of brown braids coiled on top of her head, she looked cool, regal, and too damn haughty to suit him.

Sauntering over to her he placed his arm around her shoulders. Bending down, he captured her lips in a quick kiss.

"I'm not going to let you ignore me like this," he breathed softly against her smooth skin.

He wasn't stupid. He expected a negative reaction. A scathing comeback, perhaps, or a stinging slap. But he wasn't prepared for what happened. With a broken scream she leaped up, and the top of her head caught him squarely under the chin.

Cursing, Damon stepped back. His hand flew to his bruised chin as he watched the frightened woman grope for the rail behind her. Her flailing hands finally made contact with the solid wood, and she began inching away from him.

"Stay away from me," she whispered in a panicky voice. "Stay away, or I'll call Parker."

"What the hell? What's wrong with you?" Damon approached her carefully. "Calm down. Hey. Take it easy, will you? I'm not going to hurt you." Speaking softly, his drawl exaggerated, Damon attempted to reason with her. "What is it? What's wrong?"

"What's wrong?" she squeaked, her eyes staring wildly. "You pounce on me out of the blue, maul me, *laugh* at me, and then want to know what's wrong? *You're* what's wrong, mister. I'm warning you. Go away and leave me alone, or I'll scream so loud you'll be deaf for a week."

"Okay, okay." He held up his hands placatingly. "See . . ." He took a step or two backward. "I'm backing off."

"Good," she snapped. "Just make sure you stay there." Cautiously, she inched along the rail, feeling for the stairs. "You shouldn't be let loose without a keeper," she muttered darkly. "You're a menace to society."

Damon started to protest, to deny that he was anything of the sort, when it struck him that something was drastically wrong with this scenario. It wasn't that she was wearing dark glasses after sundown. A lot of people did that. No, it was more the way she held her head. She was listening—intently—as though her very life depended on what she heard. *I've seen that particular attitude before*, he thought. *Not too long ago, either*. He raked his memory. Where? Who?

Then he knew.

"You're blind," he blurted. His taut features relaxed as he began to understand several things that had puzzled him. "I'm sorry," he said softly, his southern drawl thickening with unspoken emotion. For some odd reason he felt bereft, filled with unutterable sadness because she could not see. Why did this particular woman, with her head held high, her chin tilted upward, fill him with tender poignancy? He'd recently been closely associated with several sightless people, and they had not affected him this way.

"It wasn't your fault." She waited with resigned patience for what she knew was coming. Strangers reacted first with shock, then pity, then embarrassment when they found out she was blind. Somehow she did not sense a feeling of pity coming from this man. Strong emotions colored his voice, but pity was not one of them. "Just leave me alone," she said crisply. It didn't matter what he felt. She had to get away from him and the danger he represented.

Damon picked up the overturned chair and sat down. "That explains it," he said thoughtfully. "You weren't putting on a show for my benefit this afternoon. You didn't even know I was there, did you?"

"What difference does that make? It didn't give you license to kiss me," Christi said testily. *Nor make me come unglued!*

"Got your attention, though, didn't it?" Damon laughed lightly, like a naughty boy caught with his hand in the cookie jar.

Intrigued by the sound of his deep laughter, Christi paused in her flight. She was curious in spite of herself.

"Do you always come on so strong to any woman who happens to get in your way?" she asked seriously.

"I didn't used to. But in recent years . . ." His voice trailed off.

"Yes? In recent years?" she prompted.

"It's sort of become expected of me."

"Really?" She drew the word out while she thought about his extraordinary statement. "You must lead a *very* interesting life."

"Until now it hasn't been anything to write home about." He folded his arms across his chest and propped his feet, crossed at the ankles, on the rail. "But . . ." his voice brightened as he gazed at the woman standing before him, "things are beginning to look up." To his surprise, he was no longer bored.

He studied her intently. What *was* there about her that intrigued him? True, he had kissed her. Equally true, she had kissed him back. But, what the hell! He had kissed many women, and many women had responded to him. So? He had to admit that he didn't know why he was so interested in her. One thing he did know. He wanted to kiss her again!

"I should be very angry with you," Christi ventured after a few quiet moments passed.

"Why aren't you?"

"I don't know," she said. "This is going to sound awfully clichéd, but I don't make a habit of kissing strangers in the garden."

"I didn't think you did."

"Do you mean you still respect me?" Christi asked with a light laugh.

"Only if you promise to respect me in return," he fired back at her.

"I'll consider it," she said solemnly.

Damon felt smug. He may have behaved less than admirably this afternoon—hell, he had been a bloody bastard—but apparently this fascinating woman did not hold grudges. However, he warned himself to proceed with caution. He would have to soft-pedal his usual approach. She was still skittish, and he was afraid of frightening her away. Surprised, he realized he did not want her to leave.

"Do you live on the lake?" he asked, indicating Lake Conroe, shimmering in the moonlight, with a sweep of his arm.

"No. I'm not all that fond of water sports. I live in The Woodlands."

"Do you, now? I'm staying at the Inn."

"You aren't from around here?" she asked, more from politeness than curiosity.

"I have a place in the hill country that I call home, but I'm originally from Georgia."

"Oh. That explains the accent."

"Yes," he said shortly. He did not want to get into a conversation about his blasted accent. When he first went to L.A., fresh out of Georgia State, he was teased unmercifully about his drawl. Only in the last few years, since achieving some measure of success, had his associates decided it didn't equate with ignorance. She didn't need to know that the women in his life considered his drawl sexy.

"Are you in Houston on business?" Christi prodded.

"Yes." He was reluctant to tell her what kind of business.

"Ah. You must be in oil."

"No. Not oil, thank God. I do a little of this, a little of that, but basically, I'm just a producer. I'm here scouting locations."

What would she do now? Would she change into a brazen opportunist, willing to barter her body for a chance in one of his films? Or, wonder of wonders, would she remain the same; a charmingly normal woman who had caught his interest? He held his breath.

"Oh. 'Just a producer,' " she quoted. "Films?"

He nodded, then remembering that she couldn't see, said, "Yes."

"That explains this afternoon. You must have women coming out of the woodwork, ready and willing to do anything for a part in one of your pictures." Christi shuddered delicately. Poor man. Imagine, never knowing if you were wanted for yourself or for your influence.

Damon saw the shudder and thought she was expressing an aversion to his vocation. "All the time," he said in a hard voice. "When I saw you, reclining so seductively on that lounger, I assumed you were just one more aggressive actress trying to attract my attention."

"So you attacked," she said. She had heard the hardening of his voice and was disappointed. He was disgusted with her. She really couldn't blame him. Nice girls didn't respond to strangers' kisses the way she did to his.

"But not without provocation," he reminded her. What now? He was losing her. He could feel her withdrawing from him.

"Correction. What you *assumed* to be provocation. There was none intended. If you were trying to impress me, you went about it the wrong way."

"You're sure about that?" he prodded, enjoying the surging color that heightened her cheeks. "Where are you going?" he demanded. She was inching farther and farther away from him. "Come back and sit down."

Christi hesitated, wanting to do as he said, but fearful of putting herself in an awkward situation.

"I promise not to attack you," he said soothingly.

She gave a nervous little laugh.

"Relax. I never attack more than one unwilling woman in any twenty-four-hour period," he said with mock solemnity.

She laughed outright. Trailing her hand along the railing, she walked back to the table. Carefully feeling her way, she sat down gingerly on the edge of her chair. One hand rested on the rail. She was ready to flee if the occasion demanded.

Damon forced himself not to jump up and help her. He sensed it was important for her to do as much for herself as she could.

"I have a suggestion," he said, continuing with the conversation as though she had not almost left him.

She tilted her head in a listening attitude, waiting patiently for him to continue. Damon watched her, fascinated. Here was a woman who was prepared to listen, really listen, to him.

"I suggest we begin again," he said. "Wipe out these last few minutes. Start fresh." As he spoke the words he realized this was not just another flirtation. This was important.

He would have to examine this startling idea later, at his leisure. He was not certain he could cope with the implications now.

Damon held his breath, waiting for her answer. The sense of anticipation he'd felt earlier in the afternoon was back, stronger than ever.

"You mean, forget everything?"

"Well," he drawled, "almost everything. Some things are not meant to be forgotten."

Her low laugh was a challenge, sending shivers of anticipation dancing up and down his spine. His hands tightened around the arm of the deck chair as a current of sexual awareness raced through his large body. At that moment he knew he had to have this woman. He *would* have her.

Shaken, he reached for his melting drink.

"Who are you?" he asked in a thick voice.

"I'm Christiana, Christi, Smith," she said softly,

hesitantly, as if he should have recognized her—known who she was without her telling him.

"I'm Damon Law."

"Damon Law!" Christi's face lit up with pleasure. "I enjoyed *Evening Serenade* so much. It was one of my favorite films." Her smile faded. "I'm sorry I don't know about your more recent efforts—"

"I understand," he interrupted her. "How long have you been blind?"

A fleeting look of pain contorted her features. "Two years." Her voice echoed the pain that marked her features. "I lost my sight in the wreck that killed my husband."

"That must have been . . . Wait a minute. Smith. *Johnny* Smith?" It couldn't be . . . *she* couldn't be . . .! He dredged his memory for what he knew about the dead C&W singer's life. Dammit, she was! "You were married to Johnny Smith," he said accusingly.

Damon couldn't believe his rotten luck. The marriage of C&W star Johnny Smith had been broadcast far and wide as the love match of the century. And here he was, trying to put the make on Smith's widow. Hell, that was almost as bad as casting slurs on Snow White's honor.

He stared at her intently, wracking his brain for any scrap of information he had heard about the elusive Christi Smith. All the gossip said she lived quietly. Then what the hell was she doing at one of Parker's parties?

Was she as pure as she was made out to be, or was she involved with someone on the Q.T.? Parker? It didn't matter either way. He intended to have her. First, he must know what kind of walls he had to knock down to get to her.

"Tell me something, Christi. I'm curious. Did you really love Smith as much as they say you did, or was the 'love story of the century' just another product of some gossip columnist's fertile imagination?"

Christi stiffened as if she had been slapped. *I should be used to it*, she thought sadly. *After all this time, I should be used to it*. "I've changed my mind," she said through tight lips

"About what?" Damon leaned back in his chair and crossed his ankle over his knee. Christi could not see the slight expression of contempt that crossed his face, but the tinge of sarcasm in his voice came through loud and clear.

"I don't want to be friends with you. I want you to leave. Now." She was disappointed. For a minute she had dared to hope that this man might be different.

"Who said anything about us being friends, Christi?" he taunted softly, his drawl thickening as it always did when his emotions were involved. To hell with the kid gloves, he thought. Stick with the tried and true methods.

Ah, she thought, *he wants to play games. I don't need this*. "You were the one to suggest that we start over," she explained patiently.

"But not as friends, Christi. Never as friends." The old Damon was back, full of confidence and sure any woman was his for the choosing.

"Innuendos!" Christi closed her eyes, silently asking for strength. "I don't understand them. If you're trying to say something, do me a favor and say it in plain English."

"I mean for us to be lovers," he said bluntly. "Is that plain enough for you?"

"I see." Christi removed her dark glasses and massaged her temples. To all outward appearances she might have been talking about the weather. Inside, however . . .

Plain enough? she thought furiously. *My God! Why didn't he just hit me over the head with a two-by-four? Lovers? Him and me? Who does he think he is? What does he think I am?*

"I'm sorry, Mr. Law . . ." She continued speaking in a smooth, unruffled tone that belied her inner turmoil. "Apparently I misled you in some way."

"I don't think so, Christi." Damon could not help but be aware of her silent struggle. Her emotions were written plainly on her face for him to read. She was so serious, gathering her injured dignity and wrapping it around her in a protective cloak.

"I must have," she insisted. She felt like stamping her foot. Lord! What did it take to get through to this jerk? "I loved my husband." There was a trace of panic in her voice.

"I'm sure you did," he said placatingly. He'd better ease up a little, he thought. After all, he didn't want to drive her to hysterics.

"Oh, stop patronizing me! What I'm trying to say is that I gave all the love in me to Johnny. There is nothing left. So you see," she spread her hands in an appealing gesture, "I have nothing to offer you even if I were looking for another relationship. Which I'm not," she added emphatically.

"You're mistaken, Christi. You have a lot to offer me," he continued smoothly. It was time to hammer home his intentions.

"No, I . . ." Christi paused to gather her arguments, and Damon attacked.

"You have your mouth that tastes like honey and

makes such sweet, passionate sounds. You have a slender body with perky breasts that beg to be caressed. Not to mention your long, sexy legs that were made just to wrap around me."

"Stop it! Please," she moaned, covering her hot cheeks with her hands. "Oh, please!" Christi didn't know how to cope with this. Even Johnny, her beloved husband, had never talked to her in this dark, sexy manner.

"Yes," he said, as if it were already a fait accompli. "I will please you, Christi. Believe it."

"I'll kill Parker," she whispered into her shaking hands.

"Don't blame Parker. If we hadn't met here today, we would have met somewhere else. And soon. I'm going to bring you back to life, Christi. I'm going to be the man who frees you from the ghost of Johnny Smith."

Coming to her feet with a jerky motion, Christi reached for the railing. Her searching hands grasped the smooth wood like a lifeline, and she fled.

Damon remained on the deck for a while longer. He could see Christi, on Parker's arm, moving through the crowd. He watched them closely. Was she Parker's woman?

Parker was solicitous of her as he saw to her comfort, but Damon couldn't discern any signs of the lover about him. Parker's hand did not linger on her waist or reach out to touch her hair. There was no air of possessiveness in his attitude. Indeed, he treated her like a sister.

Parker did not seem to be in love with Christi, but what about Christi? How did she feel about Parker? He shrugged. There was time enough to find out about that later. For right now he was content to leave her in

Parker's care. However, he would see to it that he was the one who drove her home. His features hardened with determination. He would be the man who gathered her close in his arms and kissed her good night. Damon smiled a satisfied, feral smile. Tonight, at her front door, he would place his brand on her. He winced as a shriek of wild laughter cut through the evening air. And he would damn well see to it that she did not attend another one of Parker's "parties!"

He shoved his hands into his pants pockets. *Okay, Mrs. Smith, widow,* he thought. *Your life-style is about to undergo a drastic change.*

He frowned, and his hands curled into hard fists as he considered the word, "widow." It was a stark word, and the image it produced was gloomy, entirely too gloomy to be associated with the warm, vibrant woman he was watching.

He freely admitted to himself that he had no intention of changing her marital status. He did, however, fully intend to turn her into a "merry" widow. With a contented smile on his face, he joined the rest of the party.

Later in the evening Christi stood with Parker beside the pool. Though she could not see them, she knew the multicolored underwater lights back-lit exotic blooms floating on the water. Gardenias filled the air with their heady fragrance. The strong scent was slightly sickening, and Christi reeled under its onslaught. She wanted nothing more than to go home.

A shout of laughter burst over her. Several other voices joined in, swelling the sound until it filled the night around her. But they did not drown out that first deep, rumbling laugh. Damon Law's laugh. It reverberated through her body. Christi shivered.

36 / SHIRLEY FAYE

Parker felt the shiver and bent down to her. "Cold, honey?"

"No." Here was her chance to get away. "But I am tired. Will you call Billy Joe for me?"

"Aw, Christi, you don't want to leave yet. The party's just getting started," he protested halfheartedly. It had finally dawned on Parker that perhaps she shouldn't be here tonight after all. But dammit, she had to start getting out sometime, he argued with himself. She spent too much time closed up in that house, with only memories for company.

"I know," she said laconically. "That's why I think I should leave now. I don't want to cramp your style."

"Okay," Parker said, trying to hide his relief. "If you're sure that's what you want, I'll go call him."

"What's the problem, Parker?" Damon sauntered over to their group just in time to hear the last of the conversation.

"No problem, Damon. Christi wants to go home now. I'm going to call her driver."

"You mean you're not going to see her home yourself?" Damon's eyebrows rose. "In that case, I'll take her." He deftly tucked Christi's hand under his elbow.

Parker, not quite as drunk as he appeared, caught the significance of the gesture. Warily, he looked again at the big golden man standing beside him. He knew he had just been challenged.

Dammit. He didn't have time tonight to take up the gauntlet Damon had thrown down so casually. Could he leave Christi to his tender mercies? On the other hand, he'd never known Damon to go after a woman who didn't know, and agree with, the rules.

"Hey, would you? I'd appreciate that. I think I've

kept her out past her bedtime. She's worn out." The look he gave Damon said, "Watch your step."

"That's not necessary, but thank you anyway, Mr. Law," Christi put in quickly. "Billy Joe will come for me." She knew, as sure as she knew her name, that she didn't want to be cooped up in a car with Damon Law for the half-hour drive from Lake Conroe back to The Woodlands.

"It's no trouble, Christi. I'm going your way." Damon deftly slipped his arm around her waist and turned her away from the party. His steady gaze told Parker he had received and understood his message.

"Wait. My bag." Christi held back, trying frantically to think of something to get her out of this intolerable situation.

"Don't worry about it, Christi. It's safe here. You go ahead with Damon," Parker said cheerfully.

He didn't have to be so helpful, Christi thought with a wry grimace. If she didn't know better she would think he was plotting to get her and Damon together. That was impossible. He had specifically warned her to stay away from Damon. Men! Who understood them?

She walked stiffly beside Damon, trying to keep from touching him. The more she tried to pull away, the closer he held her to him.

"Relax," he murmured in her ear. "I only attack once a day, remember?"

"You . . . you're—" she stammered.

"Impossible? Arrogant? Rude? Or all of the above?" he taunted.

"Definitely all of the above!" she snapped. "And you can add dictatorial, overbearing, and bullying for good measure!"

"You'll get used to it," he said cheerfully as he

opened the car door and helped her in. "Or maybe you'd like to try your hand at reforming me?" he added. "That seems to be most women's goal in life. Reforming men."

Christi snapped her mouth shut. Why should she beat her brains out arguing with the conceited ass? Just let her get home and she would never have to suffer his presence again.

She caught her lower lip between her teeth. The prospect of never being in Damon Law's company again was not as enticing as it should be. What was she, anyway? A glutton for punishment? He had made his intentions perfectly clear, and she knew she wanted no part of him—didn't she?

THREE

Damon slid into the driver's seat and angrily slammed his door. Why did he keep picking at her? This wasn't his standard operating procedure. What was there about this woman that made him act this way?

He paused before turning onto Highway 105 and lit a cigarette. Snapping his lighter shut, he glanced at his unwilling passenger. Her head was turned away from him, as if she were staring out the window. Her arms were folded across her breasts. Her whole bearing shouted aggressive resistance. He smiled. She was a fighter. That was good. A too-easy capture spoiled the chase, and suddenly he was looking forward to this chase very much.

Christi knew when they reached Highway 105, just as she knew when they turned south onto the Interstate a little while later. The trip, which she normally enjoyed, seemed to be taking forever.

She had known back at Parker's that it would be a mistake to get in the car with Damon Law. She didn't know what the man had, but she was overwhelmingly aware of him.

She bit off a light, hysterical giggle. She had never believed in instant attraction between a man and a woman. She believed that relationships, if they were to be of any value, had to be carefully cultivated. So why did the hackneyed phrases used to describe love at first sight suddenly make sense?

Lust at first sight was what they were dealing with here, she told herself firmly. Pure old lust.

"Christi."

"What?" she yelped, as Damon's voice broke her concentration.

His low chuckle jarred her already taut nerves. Good God! He couldn't read her mind, could he? *Of course not, Christi,* she scolded herself. *Don't be silly.* She cleared her throat.

"What do you want?" The words popped out of her mouth before she could stop them. "Oh, no," she groaned. "I can't believe I said that." She dropped her head, hiding her face in her hands. She knew what he wanted. He had made that perfectly clear back at Parker's. He wanted *her*—served up on a silver platter.

Damon let her suffer as the miles clicked by. "I know you live in The Woodlands," he said finally, "but what is your address?"

"Oh." She was light-headed with relief when she realized he wasn't going to take advantage of the opening she had given him. "I live near the TPC—the Tournament Player's Course." She stumbled over directions she knew as well as her own name. It would be a miracle if he could find her house with the garbled instructions. She must have made some sort of sense, though, for a few minutes later they were pulling into her driveway.

"Thank you for bringing me home," Christi said as she reached for the door handle.

"I'll see you to your door." Damon was out of the car before she could protest that it was not necessary for him to trouble himself. She knew her own territory and did not need help here.

He opened the door and took her hand, pulling her up but not, to her surprise, into his arms. *Make up your mind, Christi,* she chided herself. *Either you want him or you don't.*

Damon's arm went around her waist as he guided her up the walk. On the porch, she turned to him.

"Thanks, again. I appreciate it," she said stiffly.

"I'll just bet you do," he laughed softly.

"If you're going to be that way, then no, I didn't appreciate it," she said, biting off the words. "I would have been more comfortable with Billy Joe."

"That's my fighter. Tell it like it is." He gathered her in his arms. "Here's something you will appreciate, though."

Christi could not see his head lower as he bent to kiss her, but she knew that was what he was going to do. Oh, yes, she knew! Even while her mind was screaming at her to pull away, her body was fitting itself to his large, muscular frame.

When his lips touched hers, she saw stars and heard bells. A fiery warmth began building low in her body, and her legs turned to water. *This is wrong, wrong, wrong,* she thought. *I loved Johnny. I still love Johnny. I shouldn't be feeling these things with this man!*

Damon broke the kiss, touched her cheek lightly with his fingertips, and left. Bemused, Christi listened to the sound of his car recede in the distance. Entering the house, she thought about moths—and flames. She had always thought the moth was a most infuriatingly stupid creature, to keep hurling itself at a flame until it was consumed.

As she made her way carefully through the house to her bedroom, Christi was feeling uncomfortably like a moth. And Damon Law was the flame that beckoned her.

The next morning, Christi, dressed in cut-offs and a bright red tank top, was swinging lazily in a hammock stretched between two shady oaks in her backyard. One bare foot hung over the side, and every once in a while she planted her toes firmly against the lush green grass and pushed. Usually she enjoyed a quiet time to herself before the day began, but there was nothing quiet about her thoughts this morning.

Upset and confused, Christi was trying to figure out exactly what had happened to her last night. Nothing in her life with Johnny had prepared her for dealing with someone like Damon Law!

Not only was Damon unlike any other man she had ever known, her own actions were so far out of character she didn't recognize herself. Christi could feel the heat of a blush creeping up her face as she recalled her behavior at her front door last night.

Her body had fit the hard angles and planes of Damon's like a hand in a glove. Everything about him had heightened her senses. The heat of his body radiated over hers with tantalizing intimacy. The strong, masculine scent that she was beginning to associate with his presence engulfed her. The whisper of his breath against her mouth just before his lips claimed hers was already familiar. Christi was aware of all these things as Damon's mouth took hers. It had not been just a kiss. It wasn't even an invasion of her senses. It was total assimilation.

Johnny, on the other hand, had spread his love over her like a protective cover, and she had snuggled under it, happy and secure. She was not being facetious when she told Damon to be straightforward with her. She knew nothing about the games played by hunting males and prowling females. With Johnny she had not needed them.

The hammock slowed to a stop while she came to grips with the fact that she had reached maturity, been married, and widowed, without ever losing her naïveté.

She had known Johnny since kindergarten. A gentle smile played about her lips as she remembered the first time she ever saw him. . . .

It was her first day at school and Christi was feeling very lost and frightened. It did not take long for the school bully to zero in on her as his first victim of the new year.

An only child, Christi was unused to normal sibling rivalry, and she was devastated by the harsh bullying. In less time than it took to tell it, the bully had reduced her to tears. When he pushed her down and dirtied her brand-new dress, it was more than she could take. Her wail of distress reached the far corners of the schoolyard.

That was when Johnny had come charging to her rescue. He dispatched the bully, picked Christi up, and brushed her off. Gazing down at her with all the superiority of a man in the third grade over a lowly kindergartener, he informed her loftily that she needed someone to look after her. He, he said, was that someone.

Furthermore, he told her sternly, she was now his girlfriend. She belonged to him and they were going to get married when they grew up.

Christi, her face tear-streaked and blotched from crying, her new dress torn and dirtied, had stared worshipfully up into his face, and nodded.

She gave the hammock a violent push. "Oh, Johnny," she sighed, "I think I need you to protect me from another bully." She scowled in the direction of a blue jay that squawked overhead, interrupting her thoughts. Even if Johnny were here, she wondered, could he protect her from her own feelings?

Johnny had been as good as his word. He never looked at another girl for the rest of his life. Even after he reached the top of the charts and was sought after by all the groupies and willing women who exist on the fringe of any entertainer's life, he never had eyes for anyone but Christi.

Christi had loved Johnny totally. He was her life, her reason for living. He was the center of her world. When he died, that world had tilted on its axis. Unused to life without him, she would have been lost even without the added burden of being blind.

Blind. She still was not used to being blind. She squeezed her eyes shut, held them tightly closed for a moment, then quickly opened them. Nope. It didn't work. For over two years she had been convinced that one day she would open her eyes, and *voilà*! her sight would be miraculously restored.

Her doctor held out a carrot of hope each time she visited him. Sometime, out there in the hazy future, there was the possibility of an operation. Sometime.

When *things* were right, they *might* be able to operate and the operation *might* restore her sight. Meanwhile, she did the best she could.

Christi was proud of her accomplishments. She'd had two worlds to learn—her world of darkness, and the real world. The world Johnny had protected her from. All in all, she had not done badly with either world.

She had learned how to navigate in total darkness. She had learned to count steps and unobtrusively feel for obstacles, both with her hands and her feet. She had learned to relax and let her instincts take over, and sense when she was close to running into an object. Yes, all things considered, she had done very well adapting to her dark world.

She also thought she had been doing well with the other, more frightening, unknown world. Until yesterday. Until Damon Law.

The strident ringing of the phone interrupted her thoughts. She ignored it. Either Peggy would get it, or they would call back. Right now she couldn't be bothered with mundane things like answering the phone. She was on the verge of facing a great truth about herself. That kiss last night was an important clue if only she knew what to make of it.

The ringing stopped, and a few seconds later Peggy called to her. "Hey, Christi! There's a guy on the phone. Says his name is Damon Law. D'ya want to talk to him?"

Christi's body went rigid in the soft hammock. What did he want? She knew the answer to that! Why wouldn't he leave her alone? Same answer. Dammit! Just hearing his name brought the memory she had been trying to push away slamming back into focus.

With an embarrassed tinge of color darkening her

face she recalled how eagerly she had put her arms around his neck, pulling him down to her. She wanted to hide from the memory of her mouth opening under the demand of his, their tongues dancing, dueling for dominance, her surrender to the surging passion Damon Law created with his touch, her moans of protest when he pulled away!

"Christi?" Peggy prompted.

"I don't want to talk to him, Peg."

"Okay." Peggy started to close the patio door, then paused and spoke again. "Chris?"

"What is it, Peggy?"

"He'll call back." Peggy snapped her gum as she waited for Christi's answer.

"Let him. I still won't talk to him."

"A battle of wills!" Peggy chuckled.

By evening Peggy was no longer laughing. Damon started calling every hour. Then he called every half hour. Then every quarter hour. The phone was now ringing every five minutes. Peggy had stopped trying to do anything but answer it.

The unfeeling instrument shrilled again.

"Chris-ti-an-a!" Peggy wailed.

"All right, Peggy. I agree. This has gone far enough." Christi yanked up the receiver as Peggy escaped thankfully into the kitchen.

"Stop this," she hissed.

"I will, now. Don't hang up." Damon's voice was first caressing, then subtly threatening.

"What do you want, Damon?" Christi demanded.

"I forgot. During the day I became consumed with an overpowering desire to prove that I can be as stubborn as you."

"You've proved it," Christi said shortly, "and almost cost me my housekeeper in the bargain. If she wasn't my friend as well, she would have been long gone by now."

"So what did you accomplish, Christi, besides wasting a whole day when we could have been together?"

"You don't take hints, do you?" she sighed.

"No. Do you know how to ride a bicycle?"

"I used to, before—"

"There's no such thing as 'used to' with bicycles," he interrupted smoothly. "It's like sex. Once you learn how, you never forget."

"Oh, rats! I walked right into that one, didn't I?" she said ruefully.

"I suppose I could have done the gentlemanly thing and overlooked the opening," he drawled in his deceptively gentle southern voice, "but you might as well know up front. I'm no gentleman."

"I think I figured that one out yesterday."

"Yes. Well. Cancel all your appointments for tomorrow, 'cause we're going riding. Be ready by nine. And pack a picnic lunch."

"But, Damon, I can't . . . Damon? Damon . . .! He hung up on me!"

When the doorbell rang promptly at nine o'clock the next morning, Christi jumped nervously, then settled back in her chair. Peggy would answer the door. All she had to do was wait and try to appear casual and blasé. It would not do for Damon to know how nervous he made her. His arsenal contained enough weapons without her adding to it.

There was a murmur of voices, then soft laughter. Now she could hear footsteps as Peggy showed Damon into the family room where she waited. He was here.

There was that scent again. Cologne, tobacco, *male*, it was more potent than any aphrodisiac. Her heart pounded and her palms broke out in a sweat.

Angry at her body's reaction to the presence of a man she told herself she didn't even like, she instinctively attacked.

"Don't smoke in my house!"

"Does it bother you, Christiana? In that case I just quit."

"Don't stop on my account. I don't care if you clog up your lungs and ruin your heart." Oh, Lord. Now he had her acting like a pouting juvenile.

"The condition of my heart should be of prime importance to you. It's all right," he said soothingly as she tried to interrupt. "Any relationship is composed of a series of compromises. My smoking offends you, so it goes. No problem. The problem, I think, is what *you* will give up in return."

"Don't hold your breath waiting to find out!" she threw over her shoulder as she heaved herself out of her chair and moved away from him.

Damon crossed to where she stared unseeingly at the golf course. Turning her in his arms, he kissed her. Christiana stiffened, then slumped against him as his lips engulfed hers and his tongue lightly teased before stealing past her lips to claim her whole mouth.

When he pulled away, Christiana rested her head against his muscular chest. Her eyes were closed and her breathing was labored.

His own breathing, Damon noted dispassionately, was not getting enough oxygen to his lungs to neutralize the lightheaded feeling that threatened to swamp him.

"Hello, Christi," he said softly. "Are you always this grouchy before you get your good-morning kiss?"

"Oh, Damon. What are you doing to me?" Christiana sighed.

"Nothing that you aren't doing to me, Christi," he said, half teasing, half seriously. "Nothing you aren't doing to me."

Reluctantly he pushed her away from him. "Where's that picnic lunch?" he asked heartily. "We're letting a beautiful day go to waste."

"In the kitchen. But, Damon, about the bicycle. I can't ride!"

"Trust me. Come on." He took her by the arm and led her outside to the driveway. "Here. See for yourself." Damon placed her hand on the handlebars of the bicycle.

Curiously, Christi ran her fingers lightly over the cool metal. Letting her sensitive fingertips send pictures to her mind, she felt down the curve of the handlebars to the rubber hand grips, then back to the neck and down the frame to the seat. Her fingers lingered over the warm leather of the seat, then drifted over the back. Here she stopped, surprised. Instead of the back wheel she expected to find, she felt another set of handlebars.

A huge smile split her face as she turned to Damon "A bicycle built for two." She laughed out loud. "Oh, Damon. Only you would think of something like this. This is wonderful!"

"Still think you can't ride a bike?" he teased, inordinately proud of himself for making her happy.

"Oh, no." Christi turned her face to the sun, inhaling the gentle early-autumn breeze. "And the weather is perfect. It's not too hot and humid to enjoy biking."

Peggy, who had followed them outside with the picnic basket, grinned impishly at Damon. Christi might have her doubts about him, but he had Peggy's full approval. He was making Christi happy. Because of him, she was getting out and having fun for the first time since the accident.

"Here ya go, sport," Peggy said as she handed him the basket and a bungee cord.

"Thanks, Peggy." Damon winked at her. "You've thought of everything."

"I tried," Peggy's gum snapped cheerfully as she winked back at him.

"I'll take good care of her, Peggy." Damon was suddenly serious.

Peggy looked him in the eye, then nodded once decisively. "I believe you. Besides," she grinned, "if you don't, Billy Joe'll break your face."

"Consider me warned." Damon laughingly backed off a step or two, holding his hands protectively before his face.

"Hey . . ." Christi called. "If you two are through talking around me as if I weren't here, can we get on with this bike ride?"

"Don't get sassy, woman!" Damon picked her up and sat her on the backseat. "Stay there and keep out of trouble while I tie the lunch down."

"By all means, secure the lunch. We must keep our priorities straight." Christi laughed. Men. They were all alike when it came to taking care of their stomachs.

Damon finished strapping the basket in place and, putting his arms around her waist, pulled her back to him. Bending his head, he nuzzled her ear. "I never lose sight of my priorities, Christi." He ran his tongue lightly around her ear. "Never." His lips grazed lightly down her cheek to her mouth, and he gave her a quick, hard kiss.

"Time to get this show on the road," he said. "Have you ever been on one of these?"

"No." Christi's reply was breathless.

Damon grinned at her agitation. She was off balance. Good. That was just where he wanted her.

"All you have to do is pedal. If you feel me braking, let up and coast. Okay?"

That sounded simple enough. She could do that, couldn't she? Of course she could. "Okay."

"Good girl. Then we're off."

The hike and bike trail in The Woodlands circled around, in and among the homes, parks, and golf courses. A long stretch of the pathway wound underneath the thick canopy of leaves formed by the many trees that gave the development its name. Then, unexpectedly, they would be out in the warm sun, skirting the edge of a golf course.

Christi was almost afraid to breathe. She hadn't felt so free since the accident. For the first time in over two years she could relax and enjoy without constantly worrying about running into something. There was no danger of her stumbling over an unexpected object. She was free to move without feeling for obstacles or counting steps. It was wonderful! Damon was wonderful!

Christi laughed, an abandoned, carefree sound that bubbled up and over, broadcasting her happiness to the man ahead of her.

Damon, hearing the joyful sound, grinned to himself. He had thought long and hard about how to spend this most important first day with Christi. He blessed the TV commercial that made him think of a tandem bike.

After a while, Damon stopped beside a pond in a small park. Three jets of water sprayed fifty feet or more into the air, falling back to the surface with a soft splash. A half dozen fat white ducks paddled contentedly in the water. Tall pines and shady oaks were reflected in the mirrorlike surface.

As in the rest of The Woodlands, the bulk of the wooded area had been left undisturbed. Thick stands of trees surrounded the pond. Underneath the trees, and spreading down to the edge of the water, the heavily matted undergrowth had been left in place.

"Oh." Christi's voice echoed her disappointment. "Do we have to stop?"

"You haven't done anything like this for quite some time, have you?" Damon asked casually.

"Nooo," Christi hedged, trying to anticipate his argument. The freedom the bike gave her was intoxicating. She wanted to keep riding forever.

"We'll stop and rest for a while. You're going to have aches in places that you didn't know you had as it is. Besides," he continued as he helped her down from the bike, "we want to do justice to this delicious lunch Peggy packed for us."

"How do you know it's delicious?" she laughed up at him. "She could have taken a violent dislike to you and packed only yucky stuff."

"No way. Peggy likes me." Damon unfastened the bungee cord and lifted the basket from the rear carrier.

"No conceit in your family, is there?" Christi teased.

"Nope." Damon hugged her to him, guiding her to a small clearing beside the duck pond. "I've got it all." He looked around. The spot was private, screened by the underbrush from prying eyes. Good.

"This will do, I think," he said. He opened the basket and smiled. Folded on top was a light blanket.

Bless you, Peggy, he thought. *With you on my side, who needs Cupid and his silly arrows?*

"Let's see what we have here," Damon said, lifting containers from the basket. "Fried chicken, deviled eggs, fresh fruit, and a tart of some kind." He rummaged deep in the basket and came up with a thermos. Unscrewing the lid he cautiously tasted the contents. "And iced tea. Doesn't sound 'yucky' to me."

"I guess you're right. Peggy likes you. I'll have you know she doesn't bake tarts for just anyone."

Damon heaped their plates, then poured tall glasses of iced tea. "Here you go, Christi. Chicken at six o'clock, deviled eggs at two, and fruit slices at ten. Here's your tea." He put her fingers around the glass, then tugged her hand down to show her where she could put her glass so it wouldn't spill.

"Open your mouth," he said, reaching back into the container.

"What? What do you think you are doing? I don't need feeding," she said indignantly.

"I know that." He picked up a juicy slice of pineapple. "Just shut up, woman, and do as I tell you."

"Well, if you're going to get radical about it." Christi folded her hands in her lap, opened her mouth, and waited. Damon leaned closer, then closer still. "Okay, now. Bite."

Christi's tongue reached out oh so carefully to touch what he was holding to her mouth. A fleeting touch, then a retreat, then a bolder touch as her senses identified the sweet fruit. With a grin, she bit down, crunching the tidbit between her teeth. Laughing, she licked at the juice that spurted and ran down her chin. Swallowing, she said, "More?"

Damon fed her the rest of the pineapple, bite by bite.

Eyeing her chin, smeared with the sticky juice, he fought a short, losing battle with himself. Muttering something that sounded suspiciously like "to hell with it," he leaned over and carefully licked the glistening juice from her face.

"Finish your lunch," he said, his drawl so thick that "your" sounded like "yo-ah."

Damon tilted his glass of iced tea and drained it in a few swallows. Leaning back against the base of a pine tree, he stared moodily at the woman across the blanket from him. Even now, in broad daylight, before God and anyone else who might happen along, he wanted her. There was no doubt about it. She turned him on.

Okay, Law, he thought. *You're in full pursuit of this woman. Now, the sixty-four-thousand-dollar question is, why? Look at her. She doesn't even come close to the type of woman you usually chase after.*

He looked her over carefully from head to toe, thinking of the cuddly, full-breasted women he normally pursued. Whatever else she is, he thought, she's definitely not "voluptuous." He ignored the little voice in the back of his head that insisted that more than a handful was wasted. *And*, he continued his brutally candid observations, *she's too thin. She'd look good on the cover of Vogue, but not in his bed*. Her legs were the longest he'd ever seen. They went on forever. He almost groaned aloud imagining them wrapped around him in passion.

He reached for the thermos and poured the last of the tea. *Think, man*, he ordered himself. *Think before you get into something you can't handle. This is not a casual woman. She doesn't play the game.*

Okay, okay, he argued, *so you're tired of the women who play. At least they're safe.*

But I don't want one of them. I want her, Christiana Smith.

She'll want the whole nine yards, he cautioned himself. *She won't settle for anything less than marriage, vine-covered cottage, babies. Commitment!*

I'll cross that bridge when I get to it, he concluded rashly.

Scowling, he remembered something he had intended to clear up before now.

"Who's Billy Joe?" he demanded out of the blue.

"What?" Christi, drowsy after the unaccustomed exercise and plentiful food, was dozing.

"Billy Joe. Who is he? Parker mentioned him the other night, and Peggy threatened me with him before we left your house. Should I run for cover? Is he going to step out of the trees with a shotgun?"

"He might, if he thought you were hurting me. He might even use it—but it would only have a quarter load and be filled with rock salt."

Damon waited patiently for her to continue.

"Billy Joe Chambers grew up with me and Johnny. When Johnny first went on the road, he went along, working as a 'roadie.'" She reached absently for another piece of chicken and nibbled on it. "Then, when Johnny needed it, he was his bodyguard. As Johnny became more and more popular, and the organization grew, he became chief of security."

"That explains what he was to Johnny. What's he to you now," Damon demanded.

"He takes care of me."

Damon stiffened. "Just how does he go about taking care of you?" he asked, his drawl thickening.

Christi almost laughed. She could see where Damon's imagination was leading him.

"Billy Joe takes care of all the things I need help with—inside and outside the house." She smiled at Damon's muttered curse. "He's my friend, Damon," she said gently, "and he's hopelessly, madly, in love with Peggy."

Damon would deny to his dying day that the giddy feeling that swept over him when he heard Christi's last statement was relief. There was no way he, Damon Law, could be that uptight over any woman's possible relationship with another man.

"You little . . ." He grabbed her by the shoulders and pushed her down onto the blanket.

"Had you going there for a minute, didn't I?" Christi giggled. "Oh, I *wish* I could see your face."

Damon held Christi's hands over her head in an iron grip and started tickling her ribs. "Lead me on, will you? I'll teach you."

"Stop," Christi giggled helplessly. "Oh, please! Stop!"

Damon stopped, but not because of Christi's pleas. The heat generated by her body pressed against his raged through him. "Little girls who play with fire get burned," he said huskily as he bent to kiss her.

Christi, dizzy from laughing, kissed him back. Once again her world tilted on its axis. Once again she was cast loose from all that was familiar and into uncharted waters. She held on for dear life to the only anchor she had. Damon Law.

FOUR

Damon's lips caressed Christi's, sliding over them possessively. He lay with one leg thrown over hers, half covering her with his big body, while he made slow, languorous love to her. His mouth claimed hers, his tongue demanded, and was granted, entrance. His free hand roamed her body, gliding over her slight curves, moving restlessly until it homed in on her breast. There it stayed—cupping, molding, kneading—until Christi made small sounds deep in her throat.

Never, Damon thought, had any woman's body fit his so perfectly. He had never known so sweet a mouth, such rapturous kisses. Christi's moans of pleasure were rewards that told him she was as excited by him as he was by her.

He broke away, looking down at her closed eyes, her swollen lips, her breasts rising and falling rapidly with excitement. He wanted her. And dammit to hell, she wanted him—whether she was ready to admit it or not.

Christi surfaced from swirling passion to find one hand around Damon's waist and the fingers of the other tangled in the thick hair on his chest. His shirt was pulled loose from his pants and almost completely unbuttoned. Had she done that? Oh, God! When? How? She didn't remember anything but drowning in Damon's embrace.

She opened her eyes. If only she could see! How many times had she wished that in the last couple of years? Countless times. Innumerable times. She would give all her hope of ever seeing again if she could only see the expression in Damon's eyes right now.

Hesitantly she reached out and touched his face. The muscles around his mouth were tense. His skin was covered with a light coating of moisture. Was it normal for him on a day as warm as today, or was it caused by the heat of passion? She moved her fingers to his brow. It was furrowed with deep lines. Were those there all the time? Or were they the result of sexual tension? She did not know, had no way of knowing, as she had not brailled him before now.

"I think," she said haltingly.

"What?" Damon asked, tracing her lips with his thumb.

"I think I should get up now," she said regretfully.

"Why?" He brushed a light kiss across her mouth.

"Why? Because, that's why." She had to restrain herself from pulling his head down for another kiss.

"It's not good enough." Damon gathered her to him, nestling her head in the crook of his shoulder.

"What's not good enough?" Christi asked, unconsciously nuzzling against him.

" 'Because.' It's not a good enough reason for me to let you go."

"How about because I want you to?"

"Want me to? Want me to do what?" Damon teased as his arms tightened around her.

"Let me go." Christi knew with anyone else she would be feeling panicky by now. Somehow, with Damon all she felt was secure. She snuggled down in his arms.

"I don't ever intend to let you go."

"I . . . why not?" Maybe she didn't feel so safe after all.

"Would you believe because I've never held a woman who felt as right in my arms as you?"

She shook her head, no.

"I didn't think so," he said, heaving a sigh.

His hand moved over her back, soothing and caressing. Christi began to feel like she was melting again, becoming a part of this dangerous man. She pushed against his chest.

"You don't really want to stop this, do you?" he asked hopefully.

"Yes." Her voice was determined, but inwardly she was wavering. If he didn't let her go soon . . .!

"I was afraid so." Reluctantly, Damon pulled away. His hands smoothed down her arms, his fingers clinging until the last minute.

For a moment Christi felt bereft, disoriented. Then, with a brisk shake of her head, she rolled over and came lightly to her feet.

"It's time I got back," she said.

"Right." Damon bit the word off short, swallowing the instinctive words of protest that rose to his lips. Damon Law had never begged for any woman's company, and he wasn't about to start now. Not knowing for sure whether he had advanced his campaign or been dealt a crippling blow, he began to gather up the remains of their lunch and pack it on the bicycle.

He whistled tunelessly as they pedaled toward her house. The notes began to take shape, forming themselves into a recognizable song. "Daisy, Daisy," he whistled over and over. When he reached the part that said, "Give me your answer, do," he realized where his thoughts were, and stopped abruptly, swearing softly and vehemently.

Damon took Christi's arm, and walked with her into the house. Peggy met them in the hall and he gave her the picnic basket. "Thanks, Peggy," he said warmly. "For everything."

"Hey, no sweat, sport." She flashed a grin at Damon as she took the basket. "Ya'll were gone a long time. Must've been havin' a good time. Chris," she turned to Christi, "Parker's on the phone."

"Thanks, Peg." Christi walked to the family room without faltering and reached for the phone.

Following her, Damon marveled. If you didn't know she was blind, he mused, you wouldn't know. Watching her confident movements, he was filled with a sense of pride in her accomplishment. It had to be terrifying, moving around in total darkness. This woman was a fighter in more ways than one. A worthy adversary.

A smile lit up her face as she spoke into the phone. God, but she was desirable! His abdominal muscles tightened with a familiar, gut-wrenching spasm. He barely registered the fact that her smile and light-hearted, teasing words were for another man. He was remembering the feel of her long, slender body under his, the taste of her mouth, the sensation of losing himself in her.

He wanted her. So much that he had to restrain himself from charging across the room, sweeping her off her feet and finding the nearest bedroom, and devil be damned!

Sauntering over to stand in front of the floor-to-ceiling windows that looked out over the golf course, he reached absently into his shirt pocket for a cigarette. Damn! He forgot for a moment he had quit. Only one day in her company and she had him so shaken he was forgetting his resolutions. It would be a miracle if the woman did not drive him to drink, or worse, before this was over!

With a tinkling laugh and a promise to be in touch, Christi hung up the phone. Turning unerringly to face Damon, she said, "Sorry. That was Parker."

"Yes. Parker." Dammit, he had just satisfied himself about the presence of one man in her life. Now he had to find out about another. And this one was dangerous. Damon shoved his clenched fist into his pocket. He realized with a start that he was doing a lot of that these days. Disgusted with himself, he took his hands out of his pockets, stretching and flexing them, trying to relax. "Let's talk about Parker Lloyd."

"No. We won't talk about Parker," she said very softly. Peggy or Billy Joe could have told him that when Christi's voice got very, very soft, that was when she was her most stubborn. Neither of them were there to tell him, though, and he didn't know. So he charged on, stumbling into dangerous territory.

"Christiana," he said tightly, "you'll tell me what Parker is to you."

Christi was sitting in an overstuffed chair, one foot tucked up under her, her nose tilted slightly upward. She was dressed in navy-blue shorts with a red-and-white-striped T-shirt. On her feet were worn Nikes. She should have looked like a little girl, with her long hair in braids. But the braids were wound around her head, and she looked very regal.

"I said no," Christi said stubbornly. "I don't talk about one of my friends to another."

Damon smiled grimly. She had inadvertently answered his question. He noted also, and filed away for future reference, that she considered him a friend, not a lover. He would have to change that—and soon.

"Parker Lloyd has a wild reputation where women are concerned. You'll stay away from him in the future." Damon stalked over to stand beside her.

"That's odd. He was just telling me the same thing about you," Christi taunted. The arrogant man thought he was going to walk into her life and start ordering her around, did he? It was long past time to disabuse him of that notion. "I'll tell you the same thing I told him. I am a grown woman, and capable of choosing my own friends."

She walked into the front hall. "I enjoyed today, Damon. Thank you," she said firmly, dismissing him.

"There you go again, Christi," he laughed, "playing with fire."

"No, I . . ." She whirled to face him, and turned right into his arms.

Damon pulled her, carefully and deliberately, against his body, tightening his arms to hold her firmly in place.

Christi pushed futilely against his chest. She might as well have been trying to push over the towering San Jacinto Monument.

"No, Damon," she moaned, trying to fight both him and her traitorous body at the same time. "I don't want this."

"Your words say one thing, your body another," he whispered, his strong arms holding her imprisoned lightly against him.

"Don't listen to my body. It doesn't know what's good for it."

Christi could feel the strong, rapid beating of his heart against her sensitive breasts. His arousal stirred against her lower stomach. She jerked, blushing, trying to pull away even as she melted against him. Drat the man! She didn't want this. She didn't!

"Oh, Christi!" he chuckled softly. "You should listen to your body. It's smarter than you."

Damon's big hand closed around the back of her neck, pulling her inexorably closer, closer still into his hard, muscular body.

Christi whimpered. She knew she was in for another one of those devastating kisses. A kiss that would make her forget everything. She would forget Johnny, herself, where she was, even the arrogance of the man who held her.

She hated it, she told herself, even as she leaned into Damon's embrace. She hated this lost, spiraling descent into passion, passion so strong and overwhelming she lost complete control of her emotions as well as her actions.

Damon heard the slight whimper. Looking sharply at her, he saw her confused state. There was both passion and pain in her expression. To his eyes, the pain was dominant. Dammit! He was driving her too hard, too fast. It was time to back off a little. Brushing a light kiss across her cheek, he gently set her from him.

"I'll see you tomorrow morning. Wear jeans."

The sound of the front door closing drew Christi out

of her daze. It took her a minute or two to realize he was gone.

Gone, and he hadn't kissed her. He hadn't taken her on another of those frightening, deliciously scary, passionate rides into oblivion. After she had braced herself to be carried away, he had left her with nothing more than a brotherly peck on the cheek!

"Oh! *Damn* the man!"

She stood facing the closed door, helplessly clenching and unclenching her fists. Then, with a small moan, she collapsed onto the antique settee in the entry hall and fought to keep from bursting into frustrated tears.

She would be damned if she would cry over the conceited ass, she thought furiously, pounding her fist against the solid oak bench. Neither tears of rage nor tears of frustration would she shed over him.

Sniffling, she swiped at her nose. Her temper began to cool, and she realized she was hurting herself, beating on the unyielding wood.

Impossible man! she thought, absently rubbing her hand. The painful bruise would be worth it, she thought ruefully, if only she had been pounding on Damon Law's thick head instead of her prized antique!

Damon was in a good mood—a fact that was apparent from the moment Peggy opened the door to his demanding knock. His booming voice echoed down the hall to the breakfast room and bounced around in Christiana's aching head.

Christi was not a morning person. For her, the day did not begin until at least two hours after she grudgingly left her bed. Damon entered the breakfast room, radiating the disgustingly cheerful aura of a person who is wide-awake when his feet hit the floor. She was strongly tempted to throw her coffee at him. Carefully, she put the still full, steaming cup back on the saucer, then turned toward him.

"Damon," Christi groaned, and got no further. Grasping her around the upper arms with his big hands, Damon lifted her into his arms for a proprietary kiss.

"Good morning, Christiana," he said, contentment oozing from him like warm syrup sliding over hotcakes.

Emotionally wrung out from trying to understand her behavior yesterday, and unable to cope with his cheerfulness so early in the morning, she croaked, "What's good about it?"

"Bad night, Christiana?" Damon asked knowingly.

"Will you put me down?" Christi said through clenched teeth. She had never been so frustrated. Here, in the flesh, was the direct cause of her sleepless night, her headache, and, for that matter, her frustration.

His tone of voice told her that he had a smug, satisfied grin on his face. Oooooh! How she would like to wipe it off! But she was trapped, trapped by the dictates of good manners that said she had to be civil and offer him a cup of coffee—to drink, not poured over his head!

Damon chuckled and let her slide back into her chair. "Finish your breakfast, Christi. I plan to cover a lot of ground today."

"Go cover it then, with my blessing," she mumbled. To her disgust, her voice was still shaky from the effects of Damon's kiss.

She reached for her coffee with a shaking hand, only to have her hand grasped in midair by Damon.

"Careful," he said sharply. "Don't burn yourself."

"Honestly, Damon!" she snapped crossly. "I managed to take care of myself quite nicely before you charged into my life!''

Christi listened to herself in mounting horror. This wasn't her. She did not know this rude, hateful woman. Since meeting Damon last Friday night, she had established a new personal record for the number of insults issued in the shortest length of time.

"I know." Damon's tone of voice, warm with admiration, defused her anger. "And a damn fine job you've done, too."

"Yes, I have, haven't I?" she said seriously, surprised at his perception. "I wouldn't have, though, if my folks and Johnny's had their way."

"Smothered you, huh?" Damon asked sympathetically as he sat down at the table and dug into the stack of hotcakes Peggy placed before him.

"You don't know the half of it," Christi groaned. "Don't get me wrong," she continued as she polished off her sausage and eggs. "They're wonderful people, and I love them dearly, but . . ." She paused.

"Yes? But?" Damon prompted.

She sipped her cooling coffee. "After the accident, no one would let me do anything for myself. They love me, and they meant well, but they wouldn't even let me *feed* myself!" she said in a burst of resentment. "As for getting about, I couldn't walk across the room without someone jumping up to guide me! And every other sentence began with 'Poor Christi.' The truly awful part was, I was just sitting back and letting them do it! It was like I had no will of my own."

"I can understand, to a certain extent," Damon said thoughtfully. "It must have been rough, losing your husband and your sight at the same time."

"Yes, it was. But no matter how bad it was, I didn't have to cease functioning as a rational adult."

"What happened to snap you out of it?"

"Parker happened, that's what." Christi laughed lightly. "He came home from Europe on one of his flying visits. It took him about five minutes to figure out what was going on. Less than a week later he had rounded up Peggy and Billy Joe and they came for me. They had me packed up and in the car before either set of parents knew what hit them."

"How did you end up here in The Woodlands?"

"Johnny and I owned two houses. This one, and one in Los Angeles. The Woodlands seemed like a good compromise with the parents. I'm not more than two hours' drive away from them, so they don't feel completely left out. It helped for me to move into a house I was already familiar with, though we hadn't had this house very long when the accident happened."

Christi paused, bracing herself for the sharp stab of pain that always accompanied thoughts of Johnny and the accident. How odd! For some reason it was neither as piercing nor as painful as she expected.

"Anyway," she continued, "you can see why I get paranoid about 'help.' "

"I promise," he intoned solemnly, "from this day on, no help. Unless, of course, you're about to walk off a fifty-foot cliff and into a nest of nasty yellow alligators."

Christi stared at him with a bemused smirk on her face.

"What are you thinking?" Damon asked, fascinated with the changing expression on her face.

"Are you sure you're a producer?" she asked mischievously. "You sound more like a writer of grade B thrillers."

"Little girls who play with fire . . ." Damon reached for her.

"Don't always get burned," Christi finished, laughing as she slipped deftly under his arm and out of his reach.

"Where are we going?" she asked a few minutes later as Damon buckled her into his vintage 1965 Corvette.

"Just wait and see, Miss Impatience," he teased.

"You're going to surprise me," Christi sighed.

"How did you guess?" Damon laughed at her woebegone expression.

"I hate surprises," she complained. "I can't stand the suspense."

"Trust me, Christiana. You'll enjoy this all the more for not knowing about it ahead of time."

A short while later Damon turned off the pavement and drove down a dirt lane.

"Come along, Grumpy," he said, opening the car door. "Time for your morning constitutional."

Christi stood beside the car, listening. She could hear bird song, and the intense quiet of a forest. In the far distance she could just make out the sound of traffic on the highway.

"Where are we?" she asked, trying to curb her impatience. Surely Damon would tell her now.

"Jones Park."

"Jones Park? You mean the little state park on FM 1488?"

"Yep." Damon put his arm around her waist and began walking. "We're going to hike the nature trail."

"Wait just a doggone minute!" Christi stopped, digging in her heels. "How long is this trail?"

"Softie!" Damon taunted. "It's not that long. You won't have time to get tired before we reach the rest area. I even brought survival rations." He tilted her chin up with his finger. "We've got all day, Christiana. Relax and enjoy it."

They sauntered along, stopping for Damon to read the plaques that identified some of the multitude of flora in the area. At each plaque he gave Christi a complete description of the tree or bush, along with a leaf or two and a small branch for her to braille.

"Won't you get in trouble, picking these?" she asked, stroking a smooth leaf with sensitive fingers.

"Would you believe I checked with the ranger station and asked if it was okay?"

"What did they say," she asked suspiciously, "yes or no?"

"I'm wounded!" Damon declared dramatically. "You have no faith in me!"

"Oh," Christi replied airily. "I have lots of faith—in you doing exactly as you please."

As they walked, Damon lifted her over exposed roots and small washouts left by heavy summer rains. Once they came to a small gully. The park rangers had mounted steps made of split logs down one side and up the other.

Damon looked at the steps, then back at Christi. It was no contest. Her desire for independence was shot down by his concern for her safety. Before she knew what was happening, he scooped her up in his arms and carried her past the obstacle.

Laughing and breathless, Christi lay nestled next to Damon's warm body, her arms linked around his neck.

This man had a strange effect on her, she thought. Only he could make her as angry as she was last night. And only he could wipe out that anger and replace it with warmth and laughter.

"I could have managed, you know," she whispered, not because she was trying to be seductive, but because she could not force a louder sound past her vocal cords.

"I know," Damon whispered back. Unconsciously he tightened his hold on her.

Christi went perfectly still. Anticipation! It was delicious. It was killing her! Would he, or would he not, kiss her? Did she even want him to? Lord, yes.

Damon felt her tense and leaped to the wrong conclusion. She was afraid of him. He was pushing too hard, too fast. Again.

Regretfully he let her slide down his body until her feet were planted firmly on the ground. Swatting her lightly on her firm jeans-clad rear he said, "Come on, woman. Time's a'wastin'."

"That's right, blame everything on me." With effort, Christi responded to his tone of voice that said, "keep it light." "And just where do you think you get off, swatting me on the fanny? Chauvinist!"

"I am not!" he said, drawing her arm through his.

"You are, too!" she teased, rubbing her face against his arm.

"Am not."

"Are, too."

They moved on down the path, bantering back and forth—determinedly ignoring the sexual tension that sparked between them.

Many twists and turns of the trail later, they came to the swinging bridge. With a darkening frown, Damon surveyed it with new awareness. He was learning to see for someone who couldn't see for herself, someone special and increasingly precious to him.

"Okay. Time to turn around and go back," he announced suddenly, swinging around and starting back down the path.

"What is it? What's the matter? What do you mean, 'go back?' We haven't come to the rest area yet. Aren't we going to stop by the creek and eat survival rations?"

"Whoa, woman! One question at a time. I'm sorry about missing out on the snacks, but I didn't know about the bridge."

"Oh. Is it washed out or something?" Christi's voice was heavy with disappointment. Darn it, anyway. She was having a ball! She hadn't been out in the woods like this for ages and ages, and now they were going to have to cut it short because of a stupid bridge!

"No. Nothing like that." Damon's answer was distracted. He had picked up on Christi's disappointment and was waging a battle with himself—her safety against her disappointment. Her safety won, hands down. He knew that. But he wanted to take away her disappointment. Dammit! He couldn't stand knowing he had done anything, however slight, to make her unhappy!

Turning her to face him, he tilted her chin up with the index finger of his right hand. He swallowed. Her beautiful brown eyes mirrored her feelings.

"It's not much of a snack, Christiana," he said soothingly. "Just crackers and cheese. And warm soda to wash it down."

Christi let out a deep sigh. At the same time her bottom lip quivered slightly.

"Oh, hell! It's a swinging bridge, Christi."

"A swinging . . . You mean it's not washed out?"

The dull film of disappointment was replaced by shining hope. Then the hope turned to sizzling anger as she realized just what Damon had been doing.

"Damon Law!" she choked, knocking his hand away, "you're *protecting* me!"

"Be reasonable, Christi. Have you ever walked on a swinging bridge?"

"No, but—"

"Doesn't the name tell you anything, for God's sake? They swing, Christi! And sway! *They are not stable!*"

"Are you talking about a bridge, or a big band from the forties?" she asked sweetly.

"Christi—"

"Is there a hand rail?" she interrupted him.

"Of course there's a hand rail," he said, exasperated that she would not listen to reason.

"Then I don't see the problem."

"That's just it! You don't see, period," he shouted.

Christi drew in her breath with a sharp gasp. Her face went white, then turned a bright red.

"Low blow, Damon," she said softly. Too softly. Then she whirled and stomped away from him. Damon watched in mounting frustration as the distance between them grew. Slowly it dawned on him that she wasn't just turning her back. She was walking away!

"Just where the hell do you think you're going?" he bellowed.

"Away from you!" she yelled back. "Just as far away from you as I can get!"

"Christi, wait. Stop! Dammit!" He reached her just before she fell headfirst into the creek. "Woman, you are making me old before my time!" He grabbed her tightly on her upper arms with both hands. He was just about to give her a good shaking when he saw the tears streaming down her cheeks.

"Hey. Don't cry, Christiana. I'm sorry. Hush now. Hush," Damon crooned, pulling her to him and rocking her gently in his arms.

"I am not crying." Christi forced the words through tightly clenched teeth.

"Oh? Could have fooled me," Damon said. His finger traced a tearstreak down her cheek. "If it looks like tears," he bent and caught a silvery drop with his tongue, "and it tastes like tears," he kissed each eyelid, "it must be tears."

"I mean, I'm crying, but I'm not *crying*."

"I see." Damon did not dare laugh. "It's clear as mud."

"I am not crying. I am mad. Angry!" she enunciated clearly.

"Christi . . ." Damon began heavily, "I'm just trying . . ."

". . . to smother me, like everyone else in the whole wide world except Parker, Peggy, and Billy Joe. I thought you understood, or were all those sympathetic words this morning just so much noise."

"Understood what?"

"How important it is for me to be able to do things for myself."

Damon ran his fingers through his hair in a gesture of helplessness. "Hell, Christi," he exploded. "I know that. I knew it Friday night."

"Then let me cross that bridge."

FIVE

Damon shook his head, trying to clear it. What had happened to their quiet walk in the woods? How had this situation reached its flash point so rapidly? And how in hell was he going to defuse it?

Troubled, he looked at the defiant woman standing before him. Then he looked over his shoulder at the bridge. Then back at Christi. Her chin was tilted at a ridiculous angle and there was a gleam of reckless challenge in her beautiful, sightless eyes. Or was it something else?

Was that a hint of fear shining past the stubborn defiance? Fear of what? Crossing the bridge? Or of failing because she had not been allowed to try? He took her face in his hands, gently turning her so he could look directly into her big brown eyes.

He saw something besides reckless stubbornness shining in her eyes. There was hope and the beginning of trust in the man who held her. Damon let out his breath in a great shudder. "Okay. But only if you promise to do exactly as I say."

Christi smiled her joy, and her whole face lit up. "I promise," she said, a little breathlessly. She, too, had sensed the importance of the situation. For one dark moment she had been afraid. Afraid that Damon would let her down. Afraid that he would revert to treating her the way everyone who did not know her did. As if her I.Q. were ten points lower than a rock because she couldn't see.

Sliding his arm around her waist, Damon led Christi to the foot of the bridge. "There is one step up, then you are on the bridge. It will not move much until you are out on it, but then it will start bouncing up and down." He placed her hand on the guy wire. "Hold this, and for God's sake, move slowly! Don't get in a hurry, or this thing will bounce you right into the creek!"

Christi put her foot out, feeling for the step. Now that she was about to get her way, she had to fight the butterflies fluttering in her middle. It was always like this when she was trying something new. Swallowing, she pushed the butterflies down and stepped up on the bridge. Confidently, she took a step forward. Her foot came down—and down.

"It slopes down," Damon said.

"Now you tell me," she laughed.

The brittle little laugh almost made Damon change his mind. Standing on the bank with his hands curled into fists at his sides, he had to make himself stay put.

The bouncing up-and-down movement of the bridge slacked off, and Christi dared to put out a tentative, seeking foot. She found the span, and stepped forward. Another step, then another.

The movement of the bridge was strange. While she was stepping down, the bridge was springing back up. It took her a couple of steps to catch the rhythm. Then, with a wide grin on her face, she stepped confidently along until she reached the lowest point at the center and began to climb upward. Again, the degree of bounce changed, and Christi, expecting it this time, changed with it. A few more steps and she was across.

Stepping down, she was on solid ground once more. For a moment, just one tiny moment, she savored her victory. Then, turning back to Damon, she said jubilantly, "I did it!"

"You sure did, darlin'." Damon's excitement matched her own. "You surely did." In a few quick strides he crossed the bridge to her side.

In a burst of exuberance Christi put her arms out and whirled around and around. Naturally, she stumbled. And, just as naturally, Damon caught her. "Careful there, Christiana." He pulled her into his arms. "Feeling your oats, are you?"

"Oh, Damon, I . . ." Christi stuttered. The heat of Damon's body, the familiar scent, the strength of his arms around her all combined with her own excitement to make her heart pound with awareness. She forgot what she was about to say. In fact, she forgot everything.

Everything but Damon.

That was Monday.

Tuesday Damon again arrived bright and early. Christi was still an early-morning grouch. He could stay, she said, if he promised not to try to engage her in conversation for at least an hour.

Damon considered it for about a split second, and

agreed. Christi heaved a sigh of relief. A moment later she was scooped up and thoroughly kissed.

"What are you doing?" she demanded furiously. "I said at least an hour, and you agreed!"

"I agreed to no talking. There were no restrictions placed on kissing."

"Ohhh. Just shut up!"

"Whatever you say, darlin'."

After sharing a quiet breakfast of Peggy's huevos rancheros they set out for Houston to spend the day at the zoo.

Christi laughed at Damon's comic descriptions of the monkeys. Then, using all his talents as a storyteller, he had her in awe of the larger animals. A delightful frisson of fear raced down her spine when he graphically described the sleek jungle cats. Timidly, she put her hand in his for reassurance while they were in the reptile house. When he kissed her on the walk beside the aviary, she sighed dreamily. All in all, it was a fun day.

Wednesday morning Christi was still slow to come to life, but she did not snap at Damon when he appeared at her breakfast table. Silently she turned her face up for his kiss, a fact that Damon noted but wisely did not comment on.

They drove east on I-10 to cross the San Jacinto River. Turning south, Damon drove for only a few minutes before stopping.

"Where are we?" Christi couldn't help but ask.

"See if you can tell me." Damon let the windows down and watched as Christi's head tilted at a familiar angle.

"I smell saltwater," she said, sniffing the air. Overhead a seagull gave a raucous cry. "Seagulls," she mused thoughtfully. She turned her face to the wind. "The wind is blowing constantly, like at the beach." She sat very still, listening carefully. "We're not at the beach, though," she continued. "There are no waves pounding on the shore, and the wind's not quite strong enough. Therefore," she said triumphantly, "we're somewhere on the bay!"

"Very good! I'm impressed." Damon was smiling at her. She could hear it in his voice. Just then an air horn across the way gave a couple of questioning toots. Another horn, very near them, answered, and the sound of powerful engines revving up split the air.

"That sounds like . . . It is! We're at the ferry! Which one, Bolivar or Lynchburg?"

"Lynchburg. I thought we would ride the ferry for a while, then eat at the sea food house on the monument side of the crossing."

"Umm. I've been there. I love their food. Let's see. This is October. Fried oysters are on the menu."

"Oysters on the half shell, too," Damon said, slanting a look at Christi.

"Ugh. Nasty things. You can have them." Christi consigned her share of the delicacy to Damon.

"Thanks." He slanted a knowing look in her direction. "Do you think I'll need them?"

"*Need* them? What . . . Oh!" Christi's face flamed as she suddenly understood what Damon was implying. "I . . ."

Damon took Christi's hand and brought it to his lips. "It's all right, Christiana. I'm just teasing. I'm not pushing you."

Christi judiciously remained silent. She had just put her foot in her mouth, and she wasn't about to risk doing it again.

That night, lying in her bed, her last memory before sleep claimed her was Damon's kiss as they stood on the surging deck of the ferry.

The sun had beat down on her head, the wind was in her face, and the salt spray flew up and over them. And again she had been oblivious of everything. Everything but Damon.

Christi lived on that kiss all day Thursday. Damon, caught up with business, did not have time to do anything but talk to her on the phone. The call came just as a disgruntled Christi was preparing for bed.

"What did you do all day, Christiana?" Damon stifled a yawn. He was weary. He had spent the day with his director, slogging his way over marshy land, searching out camera angles. He would much rather have been with Christi.

The only thing that had kept him civil these last several hours was the prospect of at least hearing her voice before the day ended. If it wasn't so late he would have been pounding on her door. The telephone, he reflected, was a poor substitute, but it beat nothing all to hell and gone.

Unfortunately, Christi mistook the yawn for boredom and his late-night call for obligation rather than pleasure.

"Oh, this and that," she said airily, determined not to let him hear anything but casual interest in her voice.

Damon stretched out on his bed. "Can't you be more specific?" he asked. His sharp ears had caught a note of forced gaiety in her words.

"Oh, I could, but . . ." Christi hedged.

"I have a feeling that I'm not going to like what you are about to say," Damon said with foreboding.

"Probably not." Christi tossed her head. "I had a visitor this afternoon."

"Parker." Damon sat up abruptly. Dammit, Christi was his. Was he going to have to blast her away from Parker Lloyd?

"How did you know?" Christi asked, not really surprised that he had guessed. For some reason Damon and Parker were acting like two starving dogs circling a bone. And she was the bone.

"My instincts are in excellent working order where you're concerned, Christiana," Damon said harshly. "What was he doing visiting you? Did you invite him to spite me? Dammit, Christi," he growled. "I told you today was business."

"Don't be silly. I don't play those games. I told you once, Damon. Parker is my friend."

"Yeah. With some friends, you don't need enemies. Don't worry, Christiana. I'll take care of him for you."

"You won't take care of anything for me, Damon Law," Christi said hotly. "I can take care of myself."

"That's where you're wrong, Christi. You're mine," he said flatly. "I take care of my own. And if that means separating you from a danger you're too blind to see, then so be it."

There was a moment of very heavy silence as Christi digested this remark. Damon, having issued his declaration, held his breath, waiting for her to speak.

Then softly, oh so very softly, Christi spoke. "Damon?" Her voice was a sexy whisper in his ear.

"Yes, Christiana?" Some of his wariness lifted. She wasn't going to explode after all.

"Will you do something for me?" The question was spoken in a soft, beguiling voice. Deceptively soft. Deceptively beguiling.

"Anything, darlin'." He was munificent in his ignorance.

"Drop dead!" she said sweetly as she slammed the receiver onto the hook.

She sat still for a moment, her chest heaving with fury. Oh, that had felt so good, slamming the phone down in Damon's ear. But, it wasn't enough. Her anger was growing, evidenced by her heaving chest and heated face. Her hand reached out. Grasping the slender telephone with a clawlike grip, she hurled it against the wall. The sound of breaking glass as a framed picture bit the dust was very satisfying. "Call me stupid, will he?" she fumed, feeling around on her nightstand for something else to throw.

She had the lamp over her shoulder, preparing to heave it after the luckless phone when the door burst open and Billy Joe stumbled into the room.

"Are you all right?" he panted, reaching for the lamp. Replacing it on the nightstand, he stared at Christi. He did not recognize the angry woman standing before him. She looked like a volcano on the verge of erupting.

"I'm fine," she bit out as she whirled away from him and began to pace. "Just fine and dandy! Tell me, Billy Joe, what's the penalty for premeditated murder in Texas?"

"Death by lethal injection. I hear it's not pretty." He pulled her out of the way just as her bare foot was about to come down on a shard of glass.

"So maybe I won't kill him. Maybe I'll just bend him a little bit," she said through stiff lips.

Billy Joe led her to the other side of the room, away from the broken glass. "Need any help?" he asked, curious about what had aroused her temper. It had to be something to do with Damon Law. But what?

"Nope," she said, eyes flashing. "I can handle this job all by myself."

"Hey, go easy on the poor guy, Christi," he said, relieved that she wasn't hurt. She was only angry.

"Are you taking his side? Against me?" She turned on him like a virago.

"No," he said, laughing out loud. It was so good to see Christi care about something, or in this case someone, enough to get mad. For so many months they had watched her just going through the motions of living. For the first time since the accident, Billy Joe allowed himself to believe that she was finally going to be all right. "I learned a long time ago to stay out of other people's fights." He paused at the door. "Just watch your step—until Peggy can get up here and clean up that glass."

Sitting on the side of the bed in his lodge at The Woodlands Inn, Damon was rubbing his ear. He sat for a long time, his face completely devoid of expression, going over and over the conversation he had just had with Christi. Finally, he began to smile. The smile grew into a grin. Then a chuckle escaped his lips. At last, he threw back his head and laughed.

By God, his Christi was a scraper. *And she was his!* The sooner she understood this irrevocable fact, the better for both of them.

He prepared for bed, still chuckling. Tomorrow he would begin settling things between them. Yes. He nodded his head once, decisively. It was past time to make Christi his, in every way.

Back in the house on Cedarwing Drive, Peggy poured coffee into two cups, then set the well-used percolator back on the stove. Sitting down at the kitchen table, she watched Billy Joe spoon too much sugar into his coffee and stir it with jerky movements. She placed a cool hand on his wrist.

"Chill out, sport," Peggy said. "She'll be fine. You'll see."

"Yeah. If I live through it. She scared the hell out of me, Peggy."

"Me, too. Big time." Peggy sipped her coffee. "But don't you see? She's alive for the first time since the accident. She sparkles. She gets mad. She . . . she *feels!*"

"Mad!" Billy Joe latched onto the one thing Peggy said that he knew was true. "I'll say she was mad! I tell you, Peggy, I've known Christi all my life, and I've never seen her as mad as she was tonight. That man sure has opened a can of worms."

"I think it's good. It's like she's been asleep for a long time. He woke her up. But," she mused, "it'll not be peaceful around here for a while."

"Maybe I should take lessons from him," Billy Joe muttered under his breath. He gazed at the coltish girl with his heart in his eyes. He knew, had known for years, that her brash, tomboyish ways were a shield she hid behind. "I sure hope she's through throwing things," he said out loud. "You'll have a helluva mess to clean up in the morning."

"Listen, sport. If throwing things makes her happy, I'll clean up behind her all day."

The object of all this speculation was doing some serious reevaluating of her own. She stepped through sliding glass doors that led from her bedroom to a closed-in deck. The deck was a sybaritic delight. Lush green plants were in every conceivable nook, scenting the air with their subtle perfume. A padded chaise, large enough for two, sat beside a hot tub.

Her movements jerky with taut nerves, Christi went straight to the tub and flipped on the switch. The water began its pulsing movement, and, a few minutes later, steam began rising in the cool night air. She shed her robe and impatiently pushed the straps of her gown over her shoulders. Letting the silky garment fall about her feet, she kicked it out of the way and stepped into the steaming tub. With a sigh, she sank into the frothing water. Leaning her head against the edge, she let the buoyant water support her body.

As sensuous as her surroundings were, Christi had never shared them with another living soul.

Her parents loved her, even if the only way they knew how to show it was by coddling her. They simply did not believe that she could function without one of them hovering over her, smothering her with misguided attention. Then there had been Johnny's family. She was the only living thing they had left of their son, and they did not intend to lose her, too.

When she left her parents' home and returned to The Woodlands with only Peggy and Billy Joe to help her, she went against all their wishes.

It had not been easy, taking charge of her own destiny, when she had been content for so long to let others lead her. The resulting battles of will often left her tense, feeling as if every muscle and tendon in her body were tied in knots.

In desperation she had the hot tub installed, hoping against hope that the hot, swirling water would help her relax so she could think clearly. Tonight was the first time in months that she had used the tub for its original purpose. Slowly, the hot, pulsing water worked its magic.

Letting her mind drift, she was horrified to realize

that in one short week she had fallen back into her old pattern of letting someone else direct her life.

That the person taking charge was a man who wanted her in his bed, rather than her overprotective parents, did not make it any better. If anything, it was worse. How had he so seduced her that she had mindlessly followed him? He was leading her closer and closer to her own fall! And what, in heaven's name, had she done to make him think of her as "his?"

True, he was a charming, if very strong-willed, man. He was certainly an attractive man. Since the day of the bicycle ride she had brailled him thoroughly and had a clear mental picture of his handsome face.

Handsome and charming as he might be, he was purely self-centered, seeking his own pleasure first and placing her welfare a poor second.

Christi was nothing if not excruciatingly honest in her evaluation of herself. She knew what she looked like. Ordinary brown hair and eyes and a tall, too thin frame. She was not the kind of woman men took one look at and pursued relentlessly. She conveniently forgot that Johnny, at the advanced age of eight, had done just that.

Johnny had loved her, and he was always telling her she was beautiful. Christi thought he had been referring to inner beauty, the kind of beauty that only getting to know a person very well reveals. Thinking about it now, she realized that she did not know, and Johnny had never said, whether he had considered her physically beautiful as well.

Damon, on the other hand, had not known her long enough to judge her inner beauty. That left only one thing. From the way he had kissed her that first afternoon at Parker's, and every day since then, he considered her only as a potential sexual conquest.

Christi had to admit that nothing in her actions this last week would lead him to think differently. Grimly she recalled the way she melted into a mindless blob when he touched her. A blush that had nothing to do with the heat of the water darkened her face. If his touch alone did that to her, his kisses—she squirmed—his kisses made her lose complete control. Even during her most intimate moments with Johnny, she had never been that far gone.

So, all things considered, there was only one thing to do. Since he only wanted her in his bed, and, since she could not control her actions when in his presence, she would not see Damon Law again.

With her decision made, Christi was aware of a feeling of loss similar to the one that she experienced when they told her Johnny was dead. Furiously, she brushed it aside. There was no comparing Johnny and Damon. It was like trying to reconcile apples and oranges. And there was no way she would admit to any deep feeling for Damon after less than a week's acquaintance. No. She had made the right decision. From now on, Damon Law was out of her life.

Christi pulled herself out of the water and padded into her bathroom for a towel. She was not looking forward to the next few days. Getting Damon out of her life would not be easy, but it could be done. She just had to remain firm.

As she dried the water from her body with a thick, velvety towel, she faced the fact that she still had one small problem. She could get Damon Law out of her life, but how was she going to get him out of her mind?

* * *

"The hell you say!" Damon's booming voice echoed down the hall to the sunny breakfast room.

Christi could hear Peggy's soft voice murmuring assurances.

"We'll just see about that!" His southern accent was thick, and getting thicker by the minute.

I knew you would be angry, Christi thought, listening to Damon arguing with Peggy. *I'll bet you've never had a woman tell you no and mean it, have you? You've always been the one to walk away. Well, Mr. Damon* womanizer *Law, the shoe's on the other foot now. How do you like it?*

Christi winced as the heavy front door slammed. Obviously he did not like it at all! Her shoulders sagged and she caught her breath on what sounded suspiciously like a sob. Damon was gone, and so was her spurt of defiance.

Taking a deep, shuddering breath, she straightened her back. She had done it. She had sent him away. Never again would she hear him call, "Hey, Chris-te-ahna," in his deep southern drawl. Never again would she know the wonder of his kisses. Never again . . .

Her head went up and her chin tilted. *Stop this, Christi*, she admonished herself fiercely. *You made your decision, and it was the right one. Stop vacillating.*

Peggy hadn't been happy when Christi told her not to admit Damon if he showed up this morning.

"Are you sure, Chris?" she had asked doubtfully.

"Yes, Peg. I've thought it over and it's best this way."

"I think you think too much," Peggy grumbled.

"What did you say?" Her mind on her decision, she heard only the tone and not the content of Peggy's words.

"Damon Law won't be stopped by an ultimatum." Peggy predicted as she set poached eggs and an English muffin in front of Christi.

"Nonsense, Peggy. Mr. Law will respect my wishes."

"On a cold day in—" Peggy broke off as Damon's familiar pounding knock interrupted her. "We'll see what we'll see," she said, going to the front door.

Now he was gone. Peggy had been wrong. Christi dropped her face into her hands. Had she been hoping that, in spite of everything, Damon would not leave? No way! She wanted him gone, out of her life.

"Eeeee!" she screamed as two brawny arms pinned her in her chair. Two large hands hit the table with a solid smack, rattling the dishes. A large body bore down on her from behind, and a familiar scent teased her senses.

"I don't know what kind of game you think you're playin', Christiana," he said raggedly, "and I haven't got time right now to find out." Big hands closed around her shoulders, lifting her out of her chair and turning her to face him. "I was going to do this differently. Take my time. Let you get to know me. But you went and changed the rules." Damon's southern accent was thick enough to cut with a knife.

His arms were bands of steel, holding her close. She could feel the tremors wracking his body. Anger? She barely had time to register that he was beyond angry and well into furious before he clasped her head with both hands.

Oh, Lord! I'm dead! Grasping his wrist, she tried futilely to loosen his hold. Expecting violence, she was shocked into utter stillness when Damon's lips brushed fleetingly against hers.

Long fingers tangled in her silky hair, holding her

still for his kiss. Lightly, teasingly, tantalizingly, he touched her lips before pulling away to launch his assault again. His tongue reached out to touch the corner of her mouth, a butterfly-light caress. She felt a slight increase in pressure as his mouth covered hers, then retreated as he gently sucked her lower lip into his mouth and nibbled on it.

Her body charged with adrenaline, her head swirling with combined fear, relief, and mounting passion, Christi sank into Damon's embrace.

Feeling her surrender, Damon deepened the kiss. All week he had been holding back, afraid to give in to the intensity of his desire. Now he pulled out all the stops. He wanted to dominate her, to possess her, to brand her. She was his, dammit, and she knew it! After today, he vowed, she would not only know it, she would admit it!

His hands slid down her neck to her shoulders. His mouth covered hers, lips moving against lips, demanding, taking, devouring. His tongue pushed relentlessly into her mouth, triumphantly claiming, subduing, caressing.

Restlessly, his hands moved on her back, blazing a heated trail down to her rounded derrière where they paused, shaping and kneading, before urgently grasping her hips and pulling her into the cradle of his hips.

Christi was vaguely aware of her soft curves fitting themselves against the hard angles and planes of Damon's big body. She snuggled against him, feeling his hardness leap into life, throbbing against her, firing an empty, aching longing in her to be filled.

Her arms slid up around his neck, pulling him down. She wanted to get closer, closer, and even closer to him. She moaned, desire and frustration mingled in the rough sound.

Damon's hand came up under the cotton knit sweater she was wearing, seeking her small, perfect breast. With a grunt of satisfaction he cupped it, holding it in his hand, shaping and stroking. His thumb brushed across the nipple, causing an immediate reaction. His fingers closed on it, pulling, tugging, creating deep, fluttering sensations that radiated throughout Christi's overheated body.

She was totally lost, her will gone, fleeing before this magnificent onslaught of passion.

Then, as on the deck at Parker's, she was alone, deserted in her moment of greatest need. With jerky, uncoordinated fingers, she felt for her chair. She found it just as her knees gave way and she collapsed, dropping heavily onto the cushioned seat.

Damon stepped back, raking shaking fingers through his hair. *"God!"* Unaware that he spoke out loud, he spun on his heel and stalked out.

Christiana jerked as the door slammed again, this time with an echo of finality. She lifted one hand, unconsciously reaching out to him. Then her hand fell lifelessly into her lap. He was gone. This time he was really gone.

SIX

It was late afternoon. As the sun reached for the western horizon, the temperature began to drop. A mild cold front was blowing across Texas. Christiana ignored the falling temperature, just as she had ignored everything and everyone throughout this day.

Again she was in her hammock, thinking. Its gentle swinging had long since ceased. Christiana was as oblivious to the motionless hammock as she was to the cooling of the evening air. Like a penitent counting her beads, she went over and over that last stormy scene with Damon.

She was in a mild state of shock, for as the day progressed, she had come to the realization that she was in love with Damon Law. When the thought first made itself known, she had repulsed it, thrust it away from her, shocked that she would even think such a thing.

But, like a bad penny, it kept coming back. Finally she gave in and allowed it to stay. Why not? she asked herself glumly. It was true. She, Christiana Smith, a blind widow, was in love with Damon Law, playboy producer.

When she admitted this to herself, many nagging questions that had been bothering her were instantly answered.

That was why she had let him into her life without an argument. That was why she had leaned into his kiss even as she told herself it was wrong. That was why he could infuriate her so.

She blinked. It did no good to understand all these things now. He was gone. She had disgusted him and sent him away. She should be relieved. Now she would not have to try to hide her feelings from him, for she surely would have to hide her love for him if Damon were still a part of her life. He was not after love and commitment. She knew this as well as she knew her name. He wanted a light flirtation, leading to an unencumbered affair. No, what he wanted could not even be dignified by calling it an affair. What he wanted was a carefree fling.

Actually she should count herself lucky. Now she would not have to worry about him divining her feelings. As casually as he had walked into her life one week ago, he had walked out of it today.

One week was all it had taken. One week to wake from her lingering grief over the loss of her husband. One week to realize that her heart was not dead. One week to learn that she was a veritable font of untapped passion . . . when she was in the presence of one large, soft voiced southerner.

Damon.

As had happened on the deck above Parker's pool exactly one week ago this evening, she could not get him out of her head. But now there was so much more to think about. She knew his humor, his thoughtfulness, his gentle touch. Last Friday all she knew was that he was a big man with a southern accent and that he could devastate her with his kisses. And she knew his scent, which she could pick out of a milling crowd. The woodsy, spicy cologne, and, above all, a male musk that said, here is a man!

It overwhelmed her, this scent that was Damon's. It clung to her clothes, her hair. It permeated her skin.

It was real! She wasn't imagining it! He was here!

She sat up quickly, sending the hammock into wild gyrations. Damon's hands caught her as she tumbled out of the hammock and they both fell to the ground, arms and legs twisted together in a lover's knot.

Christiana fought frantically to get away. Damon simply tightened his hold on her and held her bound in his viselike grip.

"Be still, woman," he said, his voice muffled against her hair.

Christiana, tense as a rabbit frozen in the headlights of an oncoming car, quieted. She was barely aware of Damon stroking her hair back from her face.

For a long time he just held her tightly against him, not saying anything. For Christiana it was heaven and hell. Never had she been so sure that she was where she belonged. Never had she been so unsure of her position.

"Ground's getting cold," Damon finally said.

"Uh huh."

"We ought to get up."

"Un huh."

He pushed himself up on one elbow and looked at her with concern. "Are you all right?"

"Un huh."

"Christiana? Christi?" He was beginning to worry about her listless responses. "I . . . ah . . . I came on pretty strong this morning."

"Uh huh."

"I didn't hurt you, did I?" Dammit! Wasn't she going to say anything except "uh huh?"

"Un uh."

Well, that was different, anyway. Damon lay back down, pulling Christiana up over him, off the cold ground. "I didn't mean to scare you, but I was so damn mad!"

"Ummm."

"Don't ever do that to me again, Christiana. Never, *ever*, try to shut me out again." His arms tightened and he tried unsuccessfully to hold back a moan. "I was so damn scared!"

That got her attention. "Scared? You?" She raised her head and stared down at him.

"Yes, me. Scared that I was losing you."

"Oh." Christiana let her head fall back on Damon's chest. She had to think about that one. She couldn't imagine Damon Law ever being afraid of losing a woman he considered his.

"I was afraid, too," she said hesitantly. "That's why I told Peggy not to let you in."

"Afraid of what? Me?" He held his breath, waiting for her answer. Why should she be afraid of him, for God's sake?

"Yes."

"Oh, no!" The whispered protest barely escaped Damon's stiff lips.

"Sort of." Christiana heard the whisper and opted for honesty. At least, she admitted to herself, as much honesty as she was willing to risk at this point. "More scared of myself, actually. Scared of how you make me feel."

"Don't ever be afraid of your feelings for me, Christi. What we have going for us is something beautiful and rare."

"I know," she said so softly Damon had to strain to hear her. "That's why it frightened me so. I'm still not . . . I can't . . . I mean . . ."

"You're not ready yet. Is that what you are trying so hard to get out?" Damon said with such warm understanding she wanted to cry.

"Yes." He understood. He was giving her time to explore these new feelings. Relieved, she sagged against him.

"Don't worry, Christi. I told you before, I'm not pushing. When the time is right, we'll both know it. Meanwhile, anticipation is part of the fun!"

Christiana laughed. A light, breathless, skittish laugh. She knew all about anticipation.

So, she thought, she knew all about anticipation, did she? It was a cinch that whatever she thought she knew last week, this week her knowledge had advanced by quantum leaps.

Christiana recalled that thought as she and Damon flew down FM 1488 in the Vette. It was a glorious day, slightly cool but bright with sunshine. The top was down, and she could feel the warmth of the sun on her skin.

Damon shifted back into high after downshifting to pass a slower car. His hand settled over Christiana's, and his fingers threaded their way through hers. He gave her a little squeeze, then just held her hand.

He was always doing things like that. Little touches on her hand, light kisses on her cheek, a fleeting caress of her hair. Little things. Caring things. Did he care for her? Or was this all an act he had perfected over the years? Did he touch her, Christiana Smith, or was he just touching a woman. Any woman?

Christiana wished for the ten millionth time that she could see his face. She missed being able to look into a person's eyes, to see the expression there. Sighted people did not realize how fortunate they were to be able to use all their faculties when judging others. She sighed.

"Steady, Miss Impatience. We're almost there," Damon said, smiling at her frowning face.

Lord, how she hated not knowing where she was going. And how he enjoyed teasing her.

"Where's 'there?' " She giggled, hearing the rhyming words. "Listen to me. 'I'm a poet and don't know it. But my feet show it.' "

" 'They're Longfellows!' " Damon shouted the punch line of the old joke with her. "Corny, Christi," he chided gently.

"See what you've done to me?" she complained. "You've scrambled my brains with all this fresh air and exercise."

During the last week, Damon had taken Christiana places she had not been to since before the accident. He had also taken her to some places she had never been. They all had one thing in common. They were outdoors, and most of them involved active, not sedentary, participation.

"You need to get out more. How'd you ever get the idea that just because you're blind you would not enjoy touring Sea Wolf Park?"

"Oh, yes," Christiana replied. "I really enjoyed hitting my head on the, whatjamacallit, bulkhead thing in that submarine. What really blows my mind, though, is trying to imagine full grown men getting about in that dinky little ship. They named them right when they called them 'tin cans.'"

"The 'tin can' was the destroyer, Christi," Damon laughed, "and submarines are 'boats,' not 'ships.'"

"Whatever." Christiana blithely waved her hand, consigning the finer distinctions between destroyers and submarines to the wind. "They're both small, with cramped space and lots of places to hit your head!"

Damon slowed for an intersection and turned north. "You don't need to worry about hitting your head today. We'll be outdoors."

"I never would have guessed," she drawled sardonically. Then she grinned. Whatever the adventure that waited for her today, she knew it would be interesting and fun. Damon simply refused to let her blindness hamper their activities.

This last week they had climbed all over the submarine and destroyer that was berthed at Sea Wolf Park in Galveston. Then, at sundown, they had walked barefoot on Galveston Beach, playing tag with the waves.

One evening they had attended a C&W concert at Miller outdoor theater. Sitting on the grassy hillside above the stage, they ate hot dogs and drank beer out of Styrofoam cups while listening to the latest C&W stars.

They had even, she remembered incredulously, spent a hilarious afternoon ice-skating at The Galleria. Ice-skating! Christiana shook her head in wonder. True, Damon held on to her the whole time they were on the ice, but she had actually skated!

At the end of each day, at her front door, he gave her a perfunctory kiss on the cheek. Then, in an aggravatingly cheerful voice, he would bid her a jaunty "Good night, Christi" and leave!

She couldn't figure it out. Here was a man who had proclaimed within hours of meeting her that they would be lovers. He had pursued her relentlessly over the last two weeks. He had kissed her *witless* last week in her breakfast room. All this time he had made it clear, beyond any shadow of a doubt, that his interest in her was purely physical. Sexual. And of the short-term variety.

Then, after hesitantly confessing his fear of losing her, he backed off. Hand-holding and brotherly pecks on the cheek did not add up, even in her skimpy book, to a playboy in hot pursuit of his next playmate.

After the second chaste ending to their day out, she had given up trying to figure him out. Instead, she resolved to enjoy his company and not worry about whether Damon still intended to seduce her. Each evening, when she drifted into sleep, the last thing she remembered was the kiss of possession he had given her in the breakfast room. Christiana trembled now in the warm sun, remembering the ecstasy of that kiss. Whether he meant to or not, Damon had branded her that day as his.

"Cold, Christi?" Damon, feeling the tremor of her hand, looked sharply at her. He caught his breath at what he saw. Christiana's face was a picture of undisguised longing and desire.

Soon, my sweet Christiana, he thought. *Soon!*

"Welcome m'lord, m'lady."

"M'lord? M'lady? Where are we?" Christiana, holding Damon's arm was dancing about with impatience.

"The Texas Renaissance Festival," Damon told her. "Hold still, Christi," he said, surveying the surging crowd. "I don't want to lose you."

"So many people," Christiana said with awe as she moved closer to Damon. "I can hear them. I can almost feel them! Listen to all the sounds! What smells so good? Food? I'm starved. Let's have some of everything! Is that a mandolin I hear? It is! They're singing a madrigal! Come *on*, Damon!"

Damon let Christiana tug him along toward the small group standing in the middle of the fairway, playing and singing their intricate, sixteenth-century harmonies.

Christiana was listening with such a rapt expression on her face that Damon, even after hearing three beautiful renditions by the group, still hesitated to leave.

"I want to stay right here," Christiana protested when he finally pulled her away.

"Okay," Damon said, "we can stay here all day if you want, but we'll miss the Shakespearean actors, the harpist, the blacksmith, the belly dancer."

"Belly dancer!" Christiana hooted disbelievingly. "You're putting me on."

"Nope. Scout's honor. There's a belly dancer gyrating . . . er . . . making her way toward us now . . ." Damon's voice trailed off as he became absorbed in watching the smooth movements of the dancer.

"Hey, Law!" Christiana snapped her fingers. "Eyes front and center!"

"Huh? Oh, sure, Christi," Damon said, momentarily distracted as his appreciative gaze centered on the dancer's well-endowed bosom. His head turned on his shoulders, watching the talented dancer until she moved out of sight.

They strolled leisurely down the lane, Damon describing the contents of each booth they passed.

Christiana examined items made of leather, pottery, silver, wood, and glass—all handcrafted and beautifully designed. She marveled over the spinner and weaver practicing their ancient crafts. She giggled at the rat-catcher's insults and laughed in amused sympathy when Damon described the men in the "stocks" being teased by the village "tart." The humor was earthy, bawdy, and laced with the speech patterns of an earlier time.

Finally, she pulled on Damon's arm, stopping him. He looked down into her flushed face. "Tired, Christi?" he asked, brushing a stray tendril of hair behind her ear.

"A little. Is there someplace where we can sit and rest for a while?"

Damon frowned, thinking of the layout of the fairgrounds. There were benches built around many of the trees that shaded the area, but they were all filled. Then he snapped his fingers. "I know just the place. Are you up to a short walk?"

"How short?" she demanded. Damon, like Parker, had conceptions of time and distance different from hers.

"Oh, about fifty yards," Damon estimated.

"Yes. I think I can walk that far without collapsing."

"More or less," he amended.

"If it's more than fifty yards, you have to carry me."

"Sure. Over my shoulder in a fireman's carry."

"On second thought, I'll manage, thank you just the same."

Damon put his arm around her waist and led her

down a byway to the Gypsy camp. It was between performances, and the rows of backless benches were deserted. Choosing a shady spot, Damon straddled the bench and pulled Christiana snug against him, her back to his front. He folded his arms around her, holding her close.

God! he groaned silently, she felt so good in his arms. So right, so . . . so . . . lovable . . .

Lovable. With an effort Damon forced the word from his thoughts. He didn't believe in love. It was an illusion, and he knew all about illusions. He dealt with them for a living.

What he had here was a clear case of wanting. Yes, he wanted Christiana. With an intensity that he had never felt for any other woman, to be sure, but it was still wanting just the same. *Don't get carried away, Law*, he warned himself. *Don't let your hormones overload your brain.*

All the time he was arguing with himself, he was nuzzling Christiana's ear. Her long hair, held back out of her face with combs, fell over his arm in silky tendrils. His tongue traced the swirls and curves of her delicate ear. His teeth nipped gently on the lobe. His attention wandered to the sensitive spot just below and behind her ear, and he tasted it to his heart's content. Then, leisurely, without haste, he worked his way down her throat with teasing, tantalizing touches of his tongue before raising his head and claiming her lips. Without his willing it, his hand made its way up from her waist to cup her breast.

It wasn't until a couple of ten-year-old boys stopped beside them, giggling and pointing, that he realized Christiana was moaning and writhing in his arms. And they were in a very public place.

Sitting up abruptly, he pulled Christiana to her feet. "Come on, Miss Impatience," he said thickly. "It's time to eat." He winked at the boys as they left the Gypsy camp. One of them, a little older than the other, grinned knowingly back at him.

Christiana walked beside Damon, but her thoughts were back at the Gypsy camp. That was the first time Damon had kissed her, really kissed her, since the scene in the breakfast room almost a week ago. The good-night salutes he had been giving her could not even be called kisses. She hugged herself joyfully. This kiss definitely was not brotherly. Damon's caresses just now had been those of a lover.

Composing her shattered demeanor, Christiana wished fervently he would make up his mind, one way or the other. This bouncing back and forth was destroying her.

After their conversation under the hammock the other evening, she was certain that it would only be a matter of time until Damon moved to become her lover. Waiting for this move was keeping her in a constant state of turmoil.

She loved him. She knew this beyond any shadow of a doubt. Damon did not love her. This she also knew. He liked her. He enjoyed her company. He went out of his way to spend time with her. Couldn't love grow from this? Couldn't he already be just a little bit in love with her? Her hopes, so high at the beginning of the week, were slowly dashed as Damon continued his strange, hands-off good-night ritual.

Now this! This almost-seduction in a public place! Christiana knew she should be embarrassed beyond words by what had happened in the Gypsy camp. But she wasn't. She was jubilant. For the first time in a long, confusing week, Damon had shown his desire for her—his uncontrollable desire for her.

Christiana grinned. Put her off with pecks on the cheek, would he? What, she wondered, had he been trying to prove? More important, who had he been trying to prove it to? Her? Or himself?

Now that she knew he was not as indifferent as he had been acting, she could take steps to end this frustrating situation. She turned her face up to the sun and laughed out loud.

"Now, why do I feel I should be threatened by that laugh, I wonder?" Damon stopped, taking Christiana's face in his hands.

"Threatened? You? A great big, strong man like you? Threatened by little, bitty me?" Christiana gurgled. She hadn't even begun her campaign and already he was nervous.

Damon's eyes narrowed in thought. She was planning something, the minx, but what?

Damon found an empty bench near the harpist's bower and left Christiana there while he purchased their lunch. She leaned back against the trunk of the tree and let the soft, mellow tones of the harp flow over her.

The mood was magical. Here, in the midst of thousands of fairgoers, with the cries of the vendors muted in the background, the harpist wove a romantic spell.

Damon returned to Christiana with great, fat sausages on sticks, *empanadas*, and apple dumplings with ice cream. They ate, listening to the tranquil music, each immersed in their own thoughts.

After lunch, Christiana began her subtle assault. She did not just hold on to Damon for guidance and security, she clung to him, turning every touch, no matter how innocent, into a caress.

104 / SHIRLEY FAYE

Damon, his senses already heightened, did not notice her hesitant touching at first. When Christiana squeezed his hand familiarly the second time in less than a minute, running her fingers up and down his inner wrist, he did notice but thought he was imagining things. Christiana, his Christiana, was not aggressive. She wasn't exactly shy and retiring, but she wasn't aggressive.

When they stopped to listen to two young Shakespearean actors emoting a scene from *The Taming of the Shrew* and she reached up to lightly caress his cheek with her hand, he began to wonder. When they walked on and she unbuttoned his shirt and ran her hand across his chest, he gasped in disbelief.

Christiana quickly bit back a grin, but not quickly enough. Damon saw, and put two and two together. The little devil, he chuckled to himself. She was pushing him!

The next time she ran teasing fingers over his face, he captured her hand and, holding it to his mouth, planted a sensual, suggestive kiss in her palm. Christiana gasped and tried to jerk her hand away. Damon just held her tighter, running his tongue up and around the beating pulse in her wrist.

The rest of the afternoon was a duel between lovers-to-be. Christiana advanced by running her hand up Damon's solidly muscled back. Damon countered by shaping her waist and running his hand down her hip. Christiana held his hand to her cheek. Damon pulled hers to his mouth, and gently sucked on her fingertips. Christiana rubbed daringly against him as they walked. Damon, standing behind her at the blacksmith's forge, pressed his arousal against her derrière.

They stayed at the blacksmith's for a very long time.

Back in the Vette, going home that evening, Christiana put her hand on Damon's thigh. He clamped his hand over hers, holding it fast. She tugged, trying to get loose. Lord, he was strong. The muscles in his legs were like iron. For the first time Christiana had some misgiving about the game she had entered into. Who was she trying to kid? She was no seductress. She was in over her head, and did not know how to swim in these unknown waters.

Damon was aware of Christiana's vacillation. He had played her game all afternoon, gently pushing a little farther than she intended each step of the way. He was curious to see just how far she would go. Did she intend to tease and run, or would she follow through on the promises she had been so recklessly making?

And she had been being reckless. Damon knew her well enough by now to know that she had no inkling of how the game was played. Obviously, then, she was not playing. Was she trying to tell him something? Was it possible that the waiting time was over? Was Christiana telling him that she was ready to belong to him? Was she, in effect, offering herself to him? If so, what exactly was she offering?

Damon shook his head. This wasn't his way, this questioning and analyzing of a woman's surrender. Why was he doing it now? Why didn't he just take what was offered and run with it?

Several miles passed while he tossed this question about in his mind. When he turned onto the Interstate, he had decided. He would take what Christiana was so sweetly offering, and, like Scarlett, think about the consequences tomorrow. He ignored the small voice in the back of his mind that was telling him he was making a mistake.

Damon and Christiana walked slowly up the driveway to her door, arms around each other, fingers clinging. Every few steps Damon pulled her close, savoring the feel of her next to him. Sexual tension arced between them like heat lightning bouncing from cloud to cloud on a summer night. When they reached the thick, carved door, Christiana turned and leaned against it.

"Good night, Damon." Her voice was soft, full of promise. "I had a lovely time."

Damon started to reach for her, then jammed his hands into his pockets. "Christiana." His voice didn't croak, exactly, but it was husky. Very husky. Clearing his throat, he tried again. "Christiana, I told you that when the time was right, we would both know."

"Yes," she said, smiling at the nervous tremor in Damon's voice. "Yes. We both know," she said softly.

"Ri—uh . . . right." He fidgeted with the change in his pocket. The tiny jingling sound was loud in the still night air. "I have a beach house down at Surf Side. The weather's still nice, not too cold yet. We could go down there tomorrow. Stay for a few days. I don't have any meetings scheduled till next Friday." Realizing suddenly that he was fidgeting with the change, he clenched it tightly in his hand.

"Okay."

SEVEN

"It's a nice place," Damon said. "I think you'll like it. Surf Side is small, but it's private. What did you say?"

"I said, 'okay.'" Christiana smiled up at him. He really was nervous. *Imagine that*, she thought. *Damon Law's nervous about asking me, Christiana Smith, to stay with him in his beach house. This has to be a first!*

"So you did," Damon said slowly. "So you did!" Now Christiana could hear a lilting note in his voice that had been missing all week. She sighed contentedly as Damon pulled her into his arms.

Turning her face up for his kiss, she slid her arms around his neck, pressing her body close to his.

"Careful there, Christi. Which one of us is pushing now?" he cautioned with a short laugh.

"I am," she breathed, pressing her lip against his, "I am."

Their lips touched, danced away, then touched again. Feather-light touches, teasing, tormenting, until they could stand it no longer. Then they melded together, bodies fusing, lips seeking, each demanding everything the other had to give.

Damon pulled her close, molding her body into his. His tongue dueled with hers, rubbing, tasting, darting about in her mouth like it was a sweet to be devoured.

He pulled away, gasping for breath, while his mouth blazed a hot trail down her arched neck.

Restlessly, his hands shaped her back, sliding down to grasp her buttocks, then moving up to her waist and back again. He shaped, kneaded, and smoothed, all the while pulling her close, ever closer, to him.

Christiana simply tried to crawl inside him. She knew that she wanted, she had to, became a part of him. Whimpering, she pulled his shirt aside, trying to get to Damon, to feel him against her, real and warm and alive.

Finally, Damon pushed her roughly away. He stood, his hands holding her shoulders while he fought for control. "I . . . I'll . . . pick you . . . up in . . . the morning . . ."

"What . . . time?" Christiana's voice, like Damon's, was slurred with the residue of passion.

"Break-fast?" Damon panted.

"Here?" Christiana gulped, slowly getting her breathing under control.

"Okay. Seven-thirty?" Damon could almost breathe normally again.

"Seven-thirty." Christiana sighed her agreement.

Planting a quick, possessive kiss on her passion-swollen lips, Damon said, "Sleep tight, Christi." Then he was gone.

Sleep? Who could possibly sleep? Christiana wondered as she listened to the sounds of his car fading away in the night.

Christiana floated up the stairs and into her room. Once there, she walked aimlessly from bed to dresser, to bath, then back to the bed again. Finally, she flopped down on her bed, on her back, with her arms stretched out above her head.

For several minutes she lay there, trying to come to terms with what had just happened. Had she really promised to spend the week with Damon, alone in his beach house at Surf Side?

Her dazed mind refused to function, so Christiana gave up thinking as a lost cause and concentrated on feeling. Lying on her bed with a silly grin on her face, she hugged herself, laughing softly.

Her mind might not be working, but her body remembered every touch of Damon's hands, every point of contact with Damon's body. Every part of her that had touched or been touched by Damon Law was sensitized and tingling.

She savored the feeling, hording it to herself, making memories to dream over. She couldn't remember when she had felt so downright good—or so exhausted. Reaching for the edge of the spread, she rolled over, pulling it with her, and promptly fell into a deep sleep.

Damon was whistling as he opened the door of his lodge. Flipping on the lights, he walked into the sitting room, tugging his shirt out of his pants as he went. He stopped dead-still when he saw Parker Lloyd sitting in the easy chair. Parker's arms were crossed over his chest. His attitude was controlled patience, as if he had nothing more important to occupy his time than waiting for Damon Law to decide to return home.

"What the hell do you think you're doing here?" Damon demanded. He was irritated but not out-and-out angry at the intrusion. The way he felt right now, nothing could make him angry.

"In a good mood, are we?" Parker said snidely. "Been cozying up to the little widow, giving her a thrill, have we? And, just incidentally, stroking your own ego in the process, huh?" Parker surged up out of the chair to stand in Damon's face. "Back off, Damon. You've had your fun. You've proved to yourself, and the world at large, that the 'ol Law charm is still in good working order."

He turned on his heel and stalked to the other side of the room. "What the hell are you doing, picking on an innocent like Christiana?" he demanded furiously as he whirled to face Damon.

"You seem to have it all figured out. You tell me," Damon said, walking into the kitchenette. He held up a bottle of Courvoisier. "How about a drink? There's no reason why we can't be comfortable while you assassinate my character, is there?"

Pouring two brandies, Damon sauntered back into the living area, gave one to Parker, then sprawled on the couch, sliding down on his spine and stretching his legs out in front of him.

Parker swirled his snifter, letting the bouquet of the brandy delight his olfactory senses. He took a sip with great care. "That's good stuff," he said grudgingly.

"I thought you would appreciate it." Damon raised his own snifter in silent salute.

"I do. But not enough to let you change the subject. What do you intend to do about Christiana?"

"I think I'll take a page out of the lady's book. To

quote Christiana, 'I don't talk about one of my friends with another.' "

"Huh!" Parker snorted. "Since when have you ever been friends with a woman?"

Damon closed his eyes while he considered Parker's question. It was a fair question. He had never thought about a woman as a friend before. "Since I met Christiana," he said slowly, surprise coloring his voice.

Parker was an astute judge of people. In spite of his anger he caught the protective body language and softening tone of voice Damon used when he spoke of Christiana. To a trained observer they told an interesting tale. Hiding a grin by tilting his snifter and draining it, he said, "Got to you, did she?"

"I wouldn't go so far as to say that," Damon said, his voice trailing off as he felt a surge of pure joy at the thought of being "got to" by Christiana.

"Just don't hurt that woman, Damon," Parker said, standing up to go. "I swear, if you do, you'll answer to me."

"Not to mention Billy Joe," Damon said solemnly.

"Yeah. Him, too."

Damon stared at the door as it closed behind his uninvited guest. How odd. He could have sworn that Parker was serious about Billy Joe! Maybe he was falling victim to Christiana's malady of scrambled brains, resulting from too much fresh air and sunshine. Shaking his head, he climbed the spiral stairs to bed.

In spite of spending the night in her clothes, Christiana woke the next morning fully rested and filled with excited anticipation. She lay still for a minute or two, thinking about spending a whole week with Damon. But, as she pushed aside the tangled cover, the enormity of what she was letting herself in for hit her. She fell back, her breath leaving her body with a whoosh. Was she ready for this? Was she really and truly ready for this?

Damon had told her, two weeks ago at Parker's, that he intended for them to be lovers. Now, with her willing help, he was about to make that prediction come true.

Two weeks. It only took him two weeks to . . . what? Storm her protective walls? Melt the ice she had been encased in since Johnny's death? Waken her from a two-year emotional sabbatical? Make her fall in love with him. Shaking her head, she got up to take her shower.

Standing under the warm water, Christiana forced herself to look realistically at Damon's actions. Was he taking advantage of her? Probably. Did she care? Of course she did. Enough to send him away? Who was she kidding. She'd tried that, and where did he go? Right into her heart, that's where.

She stepped out of the shower and dried with a fluffy towel. Did she want to go to bed with him? Yes. Why? Because she loved him, that's why. And, eternal optimist that she was, she thought he loved her, too, just a little. If she was deceiving herself, well, she wasn't doing anything that generations of women hadn't done before her.

She would go to Surf Side with Damon. She would make love with him. And she would pray that her love would be strong enough to overcome Damon's built-in prejudices against commitment. If not . . . ? She shrugged. She would cross that bridge if and when she came to it. Her decision made, Christiana went down to breakfast.

Damon was late. Seven-thirty came and went. Seven forty-five, then eight o'clock. Christiana poured another cup of coffee, then sat unheeding while it grew cold. He wasn't coming. He was tired of her. He didn't want her anymore. He'd changed his mind. He was sorry he had asked her down to Surf Side.

At five minutes after eight the doorbell rang and Damon breezed into the breakfast room, exuding his usual sexy scent, good humor—and reservations.

Was Christiana sure about her feelings? Was she having second thoughts? Did she still want to go with him? Had he pushed her too hard? Too fast?

About to greet her with a passionate good-morning kiss, Damon hesitated. He had lain awake almost all night, anticipating holding her in his arms and finally making her his. He wanted her so damn bad that if he kissed her now, he might not be able to stop. Compromising, he gave her a swift peck on the cheek.

"Good morning, Christi. Sorry I'm late. I had some last-minute business to clear up before I could get away."

"You could have called," Christiana said shortly. Her mental processes hadn't had time to switch from worrying about whether or not he was coming, when here he was, back to giving her little pecks on the cheek. And something else to worry about. Why hadn't he kissed her?

"Couldn't. I was on the phone." Damon cut into the stack of waffles Peggy sat before him, smiling his thanks at her. "Are you ready to go?"

"I've *been* ready!"

Uh oh. So that's how it was going to be. Damon looked at the woman sitting across the table from him. She was twisting her fingers together. Her face had a tight, closed look. Altogether, she did not look like a woman who was eager to be off with her lover. His confidence ebbed. She was thinking of backing out!

As he watched, her lower lip trembled ever so slightly. Damon wanted to go to her and grab her up in his arms and kiss her senseless. He clenched his fist. If he touched her now they wouldn't leave this house today.

Well, he thought, swallowing his coffee in one gulp, *I won't let her back out now. I couldn't survive if she did*. Pushing that thought to the back of his mind to be examined later, along with all the other wayward ideas he had about this woman, he stood up. "Time to go."

An hour later they were driving the coast road west of Galveston. "We could have taken the new expressway from Houston, but I like this drive," Damon explained. "That road is just another four-laned concrete monstrosity. If you've seen one, you've seen them all. Besides, we aren't in a hurry. Let's just enjoy the ride."

He took his eyes off the road for a moment to look at Christiana. She was still subdued. The happy, outgoing companion from yesterday was gone, apparently for good. Was she really having second thoughts? Did she want to call the whole thing off? Damon felt his stomach clench at the thought of not having these next few days alone with her. But, if that was what she wanted . . .

"Christiana? Do you want me to take you home?" he asked roughly.

"If that's what you want," she countered, hearing only the words and not the slight hesitancy in his voice.

"Hell, no!" he exploded. "Is that what you're sitting over there thinking? That *I* want to call it off?"

"Do you?" she asked tiredly. "I would understand it if you did."

"Why do you think I would want to do that?" he asked harshly. Christiana turned her head away from him. "Christiana! Talk to me!" he demanded.

Christiana kept her head turned away from him. Her stomach churned with nerves. She felt like she was going to be sick! Whatever gave her the idea that she could go through with this? When she had blithely made her decision this morning in the shower, she had not considered the possibility of rejection. The farther they went, the more certain she was that she was making a mistake. Damon regretted inviting her, she just knew it.

Look at how he had acted this morning. He was back to giving her brotherly pecks on the cheek! After the way he had kissed her last night it just didn't make sense! And he had acted like he couldn't stand the idea of touching her.

His actions were a clear indication to Christiana that he wanted out. Good. So did she. She was heartily tired of trying to figure him out. Anyway, she sniffed, if any rejecting was going to be done around here, she would be the one to do it. Her eyes filled with tears at the thought of rejecting Damon. Furious, she batted them back. This was not the time to be weak and weepy.

Swearing profusely, Damon turned off the paved road onto a sandy lane that led to the beach. Stopping the car, he took Christiana by her shoulders, turning her to face him.

"Now, tell me what this is all about, or I'll—" He was cut off in midsentence by the sight of one lone tear sliding down her cheek.

"Christiana, Christi, don't," he said hoarsely as he pulled her firmly to him. "Don't cry, Christi, don't cry. I'm sorry. Please, Christiana, love, please. I'm sorry."

Christiana, a casualty of her own emotional war, gave up the battle, laid her head on Damon's shoulder, and wept.

Damon, not knowing what else to do, just held her, whispering comforting words while he kissed her forehead, her cheeks, her hair.

Finally, worn out, Christiana pushed away from him, settling back in her seat. "Sorry," she said, sniffling. "I didn't mean to do that. I hate weepy women. You can take me home now."

Damon stared out over the empty horizon. The water of the gulf was a muddy gray, reflecting the overcast day. He looked back at Christiana, huddled as far away from him as she could get, and his arms, hell, his whole life, was suddenly as empty as the horizon.

"Okay," he said dully. "If that's what you want."

"It's what you want," she said in a small voice.

"The hell I do!" Damon shouted. "What gave you that cockeyed idea?"

"You did." Christiana turned her head away from him. "It's all right. I understand."

"Oh, no you don't. Not again." Damon took her firmly by the shoulders and turned her back to face him. "This time you're going to tell me what in blue blazes you're talking about."

"You didn't kiss me this morning," she said with a tiny sniff. Damon made a strangled sound. Christiana ignored him and went on, cataloging her fears. "And besides all that," she said, after telling him how worried she was that he would change his mind and how his being late had only aggravated that fear, "all morning you've been acting like touching me is simply more than you can bear."

"It is," Damon choked out through clenched teeth.

"Well, dammit! If that was the way you felt, why did you bring me out here?" Christiana waved her arms wildly to indicate the stormy beach. "Why didn't you just leave me at home to begin with?" she blurted, her hurt feelings showing more with every word.

"Oh, Christi!" Damon laughed weakly. He circled her shoulders with his arms while he leaned forward and rested his forehead against hers. "What we have here is a classic case of noncommunication. I," he turned her face up to his, "have been having a helluva time this morning trying to keep my hands off you. I was afraid that if I so much as touched you before we got to Surf Side, we'd never get there." He planted a light kiss on her stiff lips. "The only thing that kept me from sweeping you off your feet back at your house and laying you down on the nearest horizontal surface were thoughts of my nice, *private*, king-size bed at the beach."

"Oh," Christiana said in a small voice. "Then, you aren't sorry. I mean, do you still want to?"

"Yes." Damon laughed out loud with relief. She still wanted him! It was all he could do to keep from jumping up and down and shouting. "Yes, Christi. I still want to!"

He turned the key, and the vintage car roared into life. "But I want to wait until we get to the beach house." He turned and cradled her face with his hands. "I want to make it good for you, Christiana. So very, very good."

When Christiana leaned over and gave him a quick

kiss on the cheek, Damon felt ten feet tall. Grinning from ear to ear, he backed out onto the highway.

They drove on, laughing and talking. Now that the barrier of misunderstanding had been broken, there was so much to say! Nothing had been done to relieve the sexual tension between them, though. If anything, it was stronger than ever.

Damon's fingers clenched the wheel so tightly his knuckles were white with the strain. Every once in a while he would squirm and shift in his seat, trying to get comfortable. Christiana also was having a hard time sitting still. The relatively short trip became torture and they both wished, fervently, that they had taken the faster expressway from Houston.

Half an hour or so later Damon pulled off the beach road into the driveway of an A frame house set apart from its neighbors. Wanting privacy, and being able to afford it, Damon had bought the land for several hundred feet on both sides of the redwood house.

"The house faces the beach," he said, starting to familiarize Christiana with where she would be staying for the next few days. "The back entrance is directly in front of us, facing the road." He opened his door and got out of the car. "Wait here a minute."

Damon ran up the steps to the kitchen door. Opening it with a key from his key ring, he went inside and straight to the breaker box to turn on the power. Pausing only to turn up the thermostat, he went through into the living area. He was about to open the front door when he saw the fireplace.

Going over to kneel before it, he quickly laid a fire and struck a match to the tinder. Snapping his fingers impatiently, he waited for the flames to start licking at the larger wood before he replaced the screen. Looking around, he decided that everything was in order. It was time to bring Christiana inside.

Hurrying back to the car, he opened Christiana's door and helped her out. "Like I told you, the house faces the beach," he said as he led her around to the beach side of his hideaway. Turning her to face the house he said, "There are five steps up to an open porch." They walked up the steps to stand on the porch. He looked around, trying to see what was important for Christiana to know. "There are sturdy rails around the edge, about waist-high. So you don't have to worry about falling off. It's eight feet from the steps to the door." He opened the door. "Let's go inside."

Inside, he walked Christiana through the house, helping her familiarize herself with the layout and where the furniture was placed. Downstairs was the living area and the kitchen. Upstairs, jutting out over the kitchen and into the living area, was the sleeping loft and bath.

Back downstairs Damon hesitated. Suddenly, he did not know how to act around Christiana. He felt as gauche and bumbling as a teenager on his first big date. Jamming his hands into his pockets, he took them out again, swearing under his breath.

"I . . . uh . . . I guess I'll bring in our things now. Will you be all right?"

Christiana walked unerringly to the sofa in front of the free-standing fireplace and sat down. "I'll be fine," she assured him.

She made herself comfortable, listening as he went about opening up the house. If only she could help. They could work together, laughing and talking about unimportant things, like, "Where did you put the soap?" Or maybe they wouldn't talk. Maybe they would just share a comfortable silence. Either way, this strangeness they were feeling with each other would be gone, melting like snow in the warmth of their companionship.

But she couldn't help. She was in a strange place. The best thing she could do right now was stay out of Damon's way and try to find some way to get things back to normal between them before their time together was completely ruined.

In a little while Damon plopped down beside Christiana on the sofa. "All done," he reported. "Fridge is on and stocked, and the gas is turned on." He stretched his hands out to the cheery blaze crackling in the fireplace. "Fire's lit, and the house is warming up." He put his arm around Christiana and pulled her to him. "I even put fresh linens on the bed." He grinned as a delicate blush climbed up her throat to cover her face.

He felt more at ease than he had since last night at Christiana's front door. The familiar chores of opening the house had helped restore his equilibrium.

"You're very efficient," she said, relieved to hear the teasing, bantering tone in his voice. He, at least, was not uptight any longer.

"Yes," he replied smugly, "I am." He lowered his face to meet hers as he tilted her chin up. "I don't believe in wasted motion," he whispered as his lips met hers.

And just like that, their strangeness with each other vanished. With a graceful twist and turn, holding her with one arm around her shoulders, Damon lowered Christiana to the cushions.

"Very smooth, Mr. Law," she said admiringly, touching his lips with the tip of her tongue. "Do you have any more tricks like that in your repertoire?"

"Baby, you ain't seen nothin' yet," he said huskily.

"Then show me," she begged.

Damon gladly obliged. He began by planting teasing little kisses all over her face. He kissed her brow, her eyes, her adorable nose, her rosy cheeks, her slightly pointed chin. He let his tongue trail along the underside of her delicate jaw and down her throat.

Unbuttoning her blouse, he placed stinging kisses on each inch of silky skin bared to his avid gaze. Reaching the barrier of her bra, he made short work of dispensing with it, along with her blouse.

Burned forever into Damon's memory was how Christi's small, perfect breasts had felt pressing against his chest the first time he kissed her. He had been living on the memory for weeks.

He had lost count of the number of times he had told himself that reality couldn't be as good as the fantasies he'd indulged in since that fateful afternoon at Parker's. Now, with the real thing before him, he knew his memory had not exaggerated.

"Christiana, Christi, my Christi," he breathed. "You're exquisite." His mouth closed over a puckered nipple, his teeth nipped gently, then his tongue laved soothingly. "Beautiful," he murmured. "So beautiful."

His hand tugged at her slacks, and Christiana lifted her hips to let him slide them down, away from her rapidly overheating body. Damon's hand followed the material down her legs, smoothing trembling flesh, lightly running up and down, trailing fire in its wake.

Christiana moaned and moved restlessly beside him. Damon pressed a knee over her legs, holding her still under his loving exploration. His hand moved tantalizingly upward, ever upward, until it reached the juncture of her thighs. There he stopped, waiting.

"Damon," Christiana gasped as her hips arched jerkily upward. "Damon."

"What is it, Christi?" Damon's fingers made maddening little forays near, but never quite to, her throbbing flesh. "Tell me what you want, sweet Christi." He kissed her lower abdomen, tracing downward with his wet tongue. "Tell me, Christi," his husky voice was thick with emotion, his southern drawl more pronounced than ever.

"Damon," Christiana gasped again. She writhed, trying to move, trying to reach upward, to reach Damon. "Oh, God! Damon, touch me!"

Damon's fingers homed in to ease, and at the same time accentuate, Christiana's heated desire to be caressed. And all the time his fingers were working their magic, his mouth was bringing unbelievable ecstasy to the pulsing mounds that were her breasts. Higher, ever higher, he drove her. At each crest he eased off, letting her fall back a little before he began his assault again.

Christiana reached, straining, every muscle quivering with a delicious tension. Rippling waves of pleasure washed over her until, with a cry, she peaked, and fell down, down, down into Damon's encompassing embrace.

EIGHT

Christiana opened heavily lidded eyes to gaze unseeingly at the man who hovered over her. Dreamily, she smiled up at him. Sighing blissfully, she slid her arm around to his back and turned her face into his chest. It was then that she realized he was still fully dressed. She ran her hand across his chest and up his neck to cup his cheek. His skin was hot to her touch, his lips dry as he ducked his chin to plant a kiss in the palm of her hand. She could feel the strength of his arousal, pulsing against her thigh through the layers of his clothing.

"I think . . ." she sighed.

"Yes?" Damon nibbled on her fingers. "You think what?"

"I think you have on too many clothes."

"You do, huh?" Damon's lips made a foray down her arm and around to the delicate inner flesh of her wrist.

"Yes, I do. Think, that is. You are definitely overdressed for this occasion."

Damon bent down to taste her lips. They were so delicious, he went back again. And again. Pulling away, he blurted, "What do you think we should do about it?"

"About what?" Christiana mumbled, reaching up for another kiss.

"About me being overdressed."

"Oh, that. Well . . ." she drawled, "this has to go." She began unbuttoning his shirt. She let her hands run over his massive chest, fingers tangling in the thick mat of hair they found there, then moving on to tease his male nipples. She grinned when she heard his surprised gasp.

"You don't like that?" She pulled her hand away.

"Minx!" Damon grabbed her hand and placed it back on his chest. Christiana began tugging at the back of his shirt with her other hand.

Laughing and teasing, kissing each other wherever they could make contact, Christiana finally brushed Damon's shirt off his shoulders.

Damon wrapped his arms around her, pulling her against his bare chest. "Christi. Oh, Christi," he groaned. "You feel so good, so right in my arms. You fire me with your very touch, woman of mine."

His mouth covered hers as he moved his torso back and forth, teasing her nipples into hardened peaks with his fleeting touches.

"Damon," Christiana begged. "Love me!"

"I do, Christi. I am. Feel me loving you, my woman, my Christi, my love." Damon fell into a spiraling passion, only to be brought back to the present by Christi's nails scraping his stomach as she attempted to unfasten his belt buckle.

Standing up, he gathered her in his arms and turned

toward the stairs. "Come on, woman. Time to move to the bedroom and get down to some serious loving."

"What we were just doing wasn't serious?" Christiana asked incredulously.

Damon stopped halfway up the stairs and gave Christiana a swift, hard kiss. "Oh, it was serious all right. A serious appetizer. Now we're going for the main course."

"Oh . . ." Christiana snuggled against him. "I don't know if I can hold anymore."

"Yes you can, love. You can hold all I can give you."

He placed Christiana gently on the crisp sheets and stood back to strip off his remaining clothes. She felt the mattress dip as he lay down beside her and pulled her to him. Kissing her hungrily he murmured, "Christi, Christi, my sweet, sweet Christi. We've just begun to love, you and I."

Then began a veritable feast of touching, tasting, exploring, loving. Damon brought Christiana to the crest time and time again until at last he could wait no longer. Pulling her under him, he fitted his hips against hers, the pressure of his abdomen against her filling a need Christiana had not even been aware of until that moment. Gently, exercising the utmost control, Damon entered her. Then they soared. Damon thrust, and Christiana rose to meet him until they both exploded and fell from the heights together.

Damon pushed himself up on his elbows and looked at the woman beneath him. "Woman" is the key word here, he told himself. Just a woman. She was neither a goddess nor a witch, casting spells over him, making him need her, love her. She certainly wasn't the raving beauty he was accustomed to seeing in his bed. Hell, when you got right down to it, she wasn't even pretty.

The hell she wasn't.

He shook his head as if to clear it of unwanted thoughts and rolled to one side, pulling Christiana close, tucking her head onto his shoulder as he closed his eyes, reliving the last couple of hours.

Once-in-a-lifetime-loving was the thought that kept nagging at him. He tried to push the thought away. It wouldn't push. It was *loving*, and not just great sex, that he and Christiana had shared. Damon could feel the cold sweat breaking out on his brow. What the hell was he going to do now? He couldn't handle this! He didn't know anything about loving. Hell! He didn't even believe in it.

Steady there, man. Steady. Christiana hasn't mentioned love. Don't fall all over yourself babbling about something she probably doesn't want to hear. He clenched his fist. The trouble was, he wanted to say the words. He wanted to tell Christiana that he loved her. He wanted her to love him back, with all the attendant worries and woes—and pleasures and pain.

He heaved a sigh. Christiana made a little noise and stirred in his arms. He couldn't face her yet. Not now. Not when his feelings were so raw. Brushing her hair away from her face, he said, "Shh, Christi. Go to sleep now."

Christiana sighed as she snuggled trustingly against him. Damon tightened his grip, holding her close. After a lot of silent cussing and discussing, he decided to do the logical thing. He would take it slow and easy, one step at a time, feeling his way through these unknown waters. If he was very careful he could make it to the other side without slipping and falling. What he refused to think about was, what would he do when he reached the other shore and Christiana wasn't there?

He drifted into sleep, determined not to borrow trouble. Things would work out. They always did.

A couple of hours later Christiana woke to Damon's gentle caress. When she opened her eyes, he chuckled. "Oh good. You're awake."

"Only because a certain someone, who shall remain nameless, wouldn't let me sleep." She stretched, as lithe and supple as a kitten.

"Thoughtless of him. He should be taken out and horsewhipped." Damon bent his head to take her puckering nipple in his mouth and gently suck on it.

"How do you know it's a 'he?' " Christiana asked, reaching to pull Damon down on her.

"Better be a 'he.' There's no one in this bed but you and me—is there, Christiana?" Damon asked meaningfully.

"No one," she gasped as he moved from her breast up to her ear, marking his trail with light little kisses and touches of his tongue.

"No ghosts? No old memories? No anything, or anyone else?" he pressed.

"No." Christiana held his face in her hands. "No ghosts. No old memories. Nothing and no one except you. You and me," she stated firmly.

"Good." Damon pulled her over on top of him. "Now that we've got that settled . . ." He reached up and laved her nipple with his tongue, then blew quickly on it, watching in fascination as it puckered and curled in on itself. "Amazing," he murmured.

"What's amazing?" Christiana asked weakly.

"How responsive you are to me, my love," he chortled.

"Must be something in the water," Christiana said, pulling his head up for a long, satisfying kiss.

"Yes. Water," Damon muttered. "And I'm drinking at the fountain."

He flipped her over and covered her with his big body. "Christi, Christi, you're mine. You belong to me now. You realize that, don't you?" he growled. "You aren't going to fight me on this, are you?"

"I don't know. Does belonging to you mean that there will be more of what we just did?" she asked thoughtfully.

"Much, much more," he said. "Every day. All day, and far into the night."

"Then you won't get any arguments out of me, mister." Christiana gave herself up to the wonder of belonging to Damon.

"That's what I like. A compliant woman. A hot, passionate, lovingly compliant woman."

"Count your blessings, Damon Law," Christiana teased.

"I am." Damon kissed his way down from the top of her head to the tip of her toes. "I'm counting, and I intend to count thoroughly and often."

Wednesday night Christiana and Damon were sitting on the floor in front of the fireplace, popping popcorn in an old-fashioned wire popcorn popper and drinking liebfraumilch from the bottle.

Outside, the wind was howling around the eaves of the house, almost but not quite drowning out the sound of the storm-swollen waves pounding on the shore. It had been that way most of the time since Sunday night. Neither Christiana nor Damon paid any attention to it, except to hug each other a little more tightly when the wind howled sharp and loud.

Christiana snuggled down in Damon's arms, warm, happy, and secure. She would be perfectly content, she thought dreamily, if only they weren't going back to Houston tomorrow. Damon had an appointment in Atlanta with his director first thing Friday morning, so he had to fly out of Houston tomorrow evening.

She didn't want to think about Damon going away. This time, he would be back, but the day would come when he would not return. How would she ever bear it? Turning, she pressed a frantic kiss into his throat.

"Keep that up, Christi, and I'll burn the popcorn."

"Popcorn? What popcorn?" Christiana murmured. What she wanted to say was, "Burn the darn corn. I don't care. Just love me."

"What popcorn, indeed," he laughed as he tossed it aside. Damon had a brief flash of *déjà vu* as he gently pushed Christiana down to the thick quilt he had spread before the blazing fire.

He remembered sitting on the deck above Parker's pool, less than three weeks ago, telling Christiana that she had much to offer him—her sweet mouth that tasted like honey, her perfect breasts that begged to be touched, her long legs to wrap around him.

Dammit, this week was supposed to satiate his desire for this unusual creature, not just tease his appetite. He was damned if he didn't want her as much now as he did three weeks ago.

How had that happened? He had never sustained a relationship with a woman after the first, sharp desire was dulled. No matter how hard he tried—and he *had* tried in the beginning—the first hot blaze of passion was never enough to carry them through to a commitment.

But with this woman the desire grew and grew, feeding on itself. With Christiana he would just recoup from the most passionate, most meaningful lovemaking ever, only to find he had to have her again, and again. For the first time in his life Damon found himself headed toward commitment.

Sunday through Wednesday. Four days. Not enough time to bind her to him before he had to leave her for a week. The trip to Atlanta loomed over him like a giant shadow. Instinct told him to cancel the meeting. Reason told him there was no need to take such drastic action.

If only he could take Christiana with him. But that was out of the question. He would not have any time to spend with her. The round of meetings he had set up would be only wearisome. He would be dealing with an uptight assistant producer, and a director who was convinced Damon was out to sabotage his masterpiece. There would be precious little time to spend in his hotel room, and when he was there, he would not be fit company for a Viking on a rampage, much less his sweet Christiana. No. The best thing he could do would be go, get the trip over, and return, free to devote all his time to making this woman truly his.

They spent four rapturous days at Surf Side. They talked, laughed, and loved until they were exhausted, then began the whole procedure again.

They had entered the A frame on Sunday, little better than acquaintances bent on exploring a strong sexual attraction. Thursday they were lovers, but most of all they were friends.

They closed up the house, repeating their actions from Sunday. Christiana again sat on the sofa, this time in front of a dying fire, while Damon shut down and locked up.

The silence built between them like an impenetrable wall. There was so much to say. So many words trembled, unspoken, on their lips. In the end, they said nothing, neither one being able to broach the subject that lay between them.

Damon turned the Vette into Christiana's driveway. Clicking off the ignition, he sat back, drumming his fingers on the steering wheel. The closer they came to parting, the tighter the tension stretched between them. He leaned back against his door and looked at Christi huddled in her seat.

"Christi, do you want me to cancel my appointments?" Damon heard himself asking. His fingers curled into a fist and he pounded softly on the steering wheel. Before the words were even out of his mouth, he wished them back. What in the name of heaven was he doing, offering to cancel a business meeting to placate a woman?

"No, don't. If you cancel now, you'll just have to go later." Christiana's voice, small and frail as she first began to speak, became stronger with each word. "Don't pay any attention to me. I'm just being silly. But I already miss you, and you aren't even gone," she said forlornly.

Silly? She was silly? What was silly was for him, Damon Law, to be sitting here, letting this woman rope him in with her invisible, silken bonds. Silly was not saying good-bye and hustling her out of his life. Silly was listening to her talking about missing him, and being glad that she would.

Except, God help him, it wasn't silly. He knew what she meant, because the emotional wrench of leaving her was tearing him apart. Dammit, he wasn't supposed to feel these things! He had to fight this strange longing he had for Christiana Smith.

He drew a deep, shuddering breath, trying belatedly to pull his shattered defenses together. He was succeeding, until he made the mistake of looking at her.

Biting off a curse, he reached roughly for her, pulling her tightly against him. His arms were like steel bands as he held her. He cradled her head under his chin, holding her there with an iron grip on the back of her head. Her hair fell like satin ribbons through his fingers. He was dimly aware that he was losing the fight.

With a groan, he pulled back and looked at her face. Was there ever a time he had not thought she was the most beautiful of women? He couldn't remember it if there was. He took her willing mouth with a fierce hunger. A hunger that, instead of being satiated this past week as it was supposed to be, had increased by quantum leaps.

"I'll wrap this up as quickly as I can, Christi. I'll work around the clock if I have to," he promised rashly. "Whatever I have to do to get back to you as soon as possible."

"Oh, no! Not around the clock!" She feigned horror at the idea. "If you do that, you'll be so worn out when you get back you won't be any good," she joked weakly. She returned his kiss with all the pent-up frustration she was feeling.

"I'll never be too worn out for you, Christi," he said, knowing that it was true. Dear God! He could be dead and Christiana's touch would revive him!

Christiana, feverishly returning every kiss, every touch, was suddenly swamped in a tide of loneliness. Was this a foretaste of what it would be like when

Damon tired of her and went on to the next woman? Would she feel like this, all hollow and empty inside? This was worse than when Johnny died. How would she ever be able to stand it?

She wanted to wrap her arms around him and never let him go. Instead, she gathered her composure and sat back, smoothing her hair. "Do you want Billy Joe to drive you tomorrow? That way, you can leave your Vette here. It'll be safer than in the long-term lot at the airport, or even at the Inn." *And you'll have to come back to me, at least one more time.*

"Thanks. I'd like that." *And I'll have an excuse to come back to you.*

Billy Joe glanced at his watch for the umpteenth time. Striding over to the foot of the stairs, he called, "Hurry *up*, Christiana. We're going to be late!" He spun on his heel, walked back to the door, and stood there, waiting impatiently. "Women!" he muttered.

Peggy, coming down the stairs, heard him. "Patience, sport. Here she is, all spiffed up and ready to go."

Striding to the stairs, Billy Joe took Christiana's hand and led her to the car. He did not notice the result of hours of grooming and preparation. Her shining hair, brushed until it gleamed, circled her head in a crown of braids. It did not impress him. The softly tailored, antique-gold dress, teamed with a topaz necklace and earring set, was wasted on him, as were the dainty brown pumps of natural leather. As for the gold, green, and melon-colored silk scarf that was tied so casually around her trim waist, he would have snorted if he knew that choosing it was what had made Christiana late.

Peggy had patiently worked her way through Christiana's collection of brightly colored scarves, describing colors and patterns to Christi until she made a choice. Having Christiana decide what she wore and how to mix and match her clothing was one way Peggy had helped her overcome the intensive babying she had suffered at the hands of her family after the accident.

They turned off the toll road at Rankin Road and joined the line of traffic moving toward Houston Intercontinental Airport. Christiana was sitting quietly beside Billy Joe, her hands folded in her lap. But her calm appearance was belied by the brilliant sparkle in her eyes.

Damon was coming. Christiana kept repeating the phrase like a talisman. He was really coming back. To her. His plane would be landing any minute now. *Hurry*, she wanted to say, biting her lower lip. *Hurry, hurry, hurry.*

He had been gone for a week. Seven whole days. And nights. It felt like seven months had dragged by on feet of lead. Seven months? It was more like seven years, seven centuries, seven . . .

Whatever, it was seven too many.

Billy Joe drove up the spiral ramp to the rooftop parking lot. Taking Christiana's arm, he led her to the elevator and pushed the button. He had a feeling that the 747 taxiing up to the building now was the flight they were here to meet. He jabbed at the button again, willing the slow-moving car to hurry. He hated to be late.

He had tried to talk Christiana into waiting at home, but that had been a lost cause before he even got started. Stubbornly, she insisted on coming with him to meet Damon.

What had happened? he wondered. She was only

supposed to get out and have some fun. She wasn't supposed to get so serious about this man. I mean, hell, he had argued with Peggy and Parker, not only was Damon the first man she had been involved with since Johnny's death, he was the only man, besides Johnny, she had ever gone out with.

He bit off a rough expletive. In his opinion, Christiana was in too deep. Lord! Who would have thought she would fall for someone like Damon Law?

Parker insisted that there was nothing to worry about, but Billy Joe wasn't so sure. He had a bad feeling about this playboy producer. This whole thing had happened too fast. Billy Joe was another believer in slow and sure. Look how long he had been courting Peggy.

He was afraid, in spite of Parker's reassurance to the contrary, that Law would end up hurting Christiana. It was not the bachelor playboy's way to settle down with one woman. Christiana was cruising for a bruising, and there was nothing he, Billy Joe, could about it. Nothing, that is, except be there to help pick up the pieces when it was all over.

In Billy Joe's opinion, there would be lots of pieces. Christiana was fragile, and she would shatter. Before this affair reached its natural conclusion, Damon Law would crush her. He just hoped that he would not do such a thorough job of it that he, Peggy, and Parker could not pick up the pieces and put Christi back together—again.

The slow-moving elevator finally stopped, and they walked down the concourse. To Billy Joe's surprise, they were in time. The passengers from Atlanta were just beginning to deplane.

Damon waited until the first rush of passengers pushed and shoved their way through the first-class compartment. Then, standing and stretching his cramped legs, he picked up his briefcase, smiled absently at the flight attendant, and stepped out of the plane. The empty jetway stretched before him when he looked up and saw Christiana, a vision in gold, waiting. For him. Like water rolling off a duck's back, his weariness fell from his shoulders. Grinning from ear to ear, he quickened his step. By the time he reached her, he was almost running.

Picking her up, he whirled her around and hugged her to him. God! She felt so good! The tediousness and frustrations of the last week disappeared, and in its place was a surging awareness of the woman he held in his arms.

"Hello-Christi-God-I-missed-you," he said, running his words together as he bent to kiss her.

Christiana gave herself up to his passionate greeting. She had recognized Damon by his distinctive scent even before he touched her. Crowds of people surged around them, but she didn't care. They could have been standing in the middle of the freeway during the rush hour and she would not have cared. All she cared about was being where she was. In Damon's arms.

His lips moved on hers, twisting to open her mouth for his possessive tongue. Christiana lost all awareness. The milling people, the hollow voice on the loudspeaker, everything faded away. Her hands ran up under his suit coat, over his massive chest to circle around the back of his neck and tangle in his hair. Her body molded to him as if finding the other part of itself. She told him without words just how much she had missed him, how lonely she had been without him, and how deliriously happy she was that he was back.

"Whoeee, Christi. Are you trying to tell me something?" Damon broke away, breathing deeply.

Christiana laughed. A clear, ringing sound of pure happiness. "I sure am," she grinned saucily. "Are you getting the message?"

"Received and understood, love." He leaned down to her, loving the scent of her, the feel of her, everything about her. "Missed me, huh?"

Stifling a happy burst of laughter at the obvious, Christiana nodded her head. "Are you ready to go?"

"Yes." He looked around for his briefcase, only to see Billy Joe holding it up. He grinned at the security chief turned handyman. "Thank you," he said. His eyes held Billy Joe's for a moment, emphasizing his words, and saying so much more.

Billy Joe just grunted. "If you'll give me your claim ticket, I'll get your cases. You can take Christiana to the car. It's on the roof, just outside the elevator." He tossed the keys to Damon and took the claim ticket.

Watching Christiana and Damon walk to the elevator, arms wrapped around each other, Billy Joe shook his head. He still did not feel comfortable with this situation. If he read the signs correctly, Damon Law had just told him he was worrying needlessly. But Christiana, for all the fact that she was a widow, was a babe in the woods when it came to handling sophisticated relationships.

He just knew one thing for sure, he thought, getting on the escalator to go down to the baggage claim area. If that slick-talkin' dude ever hurt her, he would answer to Billy Joe Chambers.

An hour later, a disgruntled Billy Joe left Christiana with Damon in his lodge at The Woodlands Inn. Impervious to his disapproval, Christiana could hardly wait for him to leave.

After taking Damon's case up the spiral staircase to the sleeping loft, Billy Joe had waited around hopefully for Christiana to say good-bye and come home where she belonged. A short minute later, however, he found himself outside, listening to the click of the bolt as the door was locked firmly in his face. Driving back to Cedarwing Drive, he grinned ruefully to himself. He had sure as hell lost that round.

NINE

"My, my, my," Christiana said admiringly as Damon came back into the living area after bolting the door. "You handled that nicely. Slick as goose grease, if I do say so myself."

"Huh!" Damon grumbled. "Thick-headed idiot. I thought for a minute I was going to have to push him out the door. Do you inspire such protective loyalty in all your friends, my Christi? Am I going to have to battle my way past each and every one of them to get to you?"

"Possibly," Christiana replied. "They have been very helpful, very protective of me since the accident. They care about me."

Damon pulled her to him, growling possessively as he lowered his mouth to hers. "I care about you, too," he said. "And I'll fight my way through whole battalions if necessary." His lips pressed against hers, claiming, possessing, branding, while at the same time caressing them lovingly. His tongue reached out to trace her lower lip slowly, reacquainting itself with its contours and taste. "Open your mouth to me, Christi," he whispered. "I've been so cold and lonely without you. Let me in, love. Let me come home."

"Ah, Damon," Christiana sighed. "I've missed you. Hold me," she cried, tightening her arms around him when she thought his grip was loosening. "Please. Hold me." She turned her face back to his, reaching again for his kiss, giving herself up to the pleasure of being in the arms of the man she loved.

An eternity later they surfaced for air. Christiana's neat braids were hanging, half unraveled, down her back. Her dress was unbuttoned, and the colorful scarf, chosen with such care, lay on the floor. She had kicked off her shoes and was standing on tiptoe, her arms wound tightly around Damon's neck, pulling his head down to her.

Damon also looked like a survivor of a war zone. His suit jacket lay where it had landed, somewhere near the coffee table. His hair was rumpled and his tie was loosened and pulled to one side. His shirt was completely unbuttoned and hung half in and half out of his neatly tailored suit pants. There was a smear of Christiana's lipstick still visible on the corner of his mouth.

He held her tightly to him as his glazed eyes focused on the narrow spiral staircase in the corner of the room. The way he felt, perhaps it was just as well he couldn't possibly carry Christiana up the narrow stairs. Chuckling softly at the irony of a woman's kiss making his legs turn to rubber, he tilted her face up to his. "Christi, can you walk?"

"Walk?" Christiana repeated, bemused. She was

still dizzy, her brain still mush, from the passionate embrace. What was Damon talking about?

"Up the stairs. If you want to continue this in the comfort of my bed, you'll have to go up under your own steam."

"If it's steam you need, you're talking to the right person," she said. "I'm definitely steaming."

Damon let out a shout of laughter. "Oh, Christi. You might not have understood innuendoes when we first met, but you're learning."

"Good, huh?" Christiana smirked, tickled at having made Damon laugh.

"Passable." Damon touched her cheek with his fingertips, acknowledging her successful attempt at cracking a joke. "Just don't get carried away."

"I can't." Christiana reached up and brushed his lips with hers. "You just told me I had to walk."

"Move, woman!" Damon swatted her on the behind and turned her toward the stairs.

"Much more of that," Christiana said, rubbing her rear, "and I'll move all right. Right out the front door."

"Try it and see how far you get," Damon said, half teasingly, half threateningly.

"Would you really keep me from leaving?" Christiana asked, half believing his threat.

"I'll keep you, period," Damon stated flatly. "You're mine, Christi, and I don't ever intend to let you go."

This wasn't the first time Damon had claimed that she was his, Christiana thought as she climbed the stairs. He had been saying it since that first day they spent together. But it was the first time Christiana let herself believe, just a little, that he meant what he was saying. There was a quality to his voice that said he was speaking the truth.

Upstairs, Damon turned down the covers on the king-size bed. Christiana sat on the foot of the bed, running her fingers through her braids, finishing the unraveling process started by Damon downstairs. The glossy strands of hair fell loosely around her shoulders.

Damon looked at her, his breath catching in his throat. She was so entrancing. And she loved him.

He froze, knowing he had stumbled on a truth. Christiana had never told him with words that she loved him. But, he realized, she had told him in so many other ways. He knew now, without her ever saying it, that when she gave him the gift of her body, she had also placed her heart in his hands.

Grimly, he looked down at his big hands, turning them over and over, looking at them as if he had never seen them before. They were so large, so competent. They could hold her heart safely—or crush it with one thoughtless move. He clenched and unclenched his fist, watching it open and close. It was frightening to be the possible bearer of so much pain and heartbreak.

He made a silent vow to the trusting woman sitting at the foot of his bed. He promised he would never willfully, never knowingly, do anything to hurt her. Just how he was going to accomplish this and retain his freedom, he did not know. He would think about it later.

Christiana stretched, letting her dress fall to the floor. Her other clothing quickly followed. God, he thought, she was beautiful. How had he ever thought she was not? How had he become so cynical that he had not seen past physical imperfection to the beauty within before now? How had he failed to recognize, right off the bat, that she was worth so much more than any other woman he had known?

Picking up his hairbrush, he went to her. "Here," he said roughly. "Let me."

Gently he pushed her down to sit on the floor and took his place behind her on the edge of the bed. His legs closed protectively around each side of her slender body as he began brushing her hair. His strokes were long and sensual. Again and again he placed the brush on the crown of her head and slowly pulled it through the silky brown strands.

Heat flamed around them, engulfing them, growing with each stroke of the brush. Just when she thought she could not stand it for another minute, Christiana felt Damon's fingers on her chin as he gently turned her to him. He bent to her slowly, slowly, so that she felt his breath tickling her lips long before his claimed hers.

With a twist of his mouth, Damon deepened the kiss. His tongue reached out to sweep her mouth with a thoroughness that knew no bounds. Christiana, trying to keep up with the darting thrust, soon felt faint with desire.

No, no, she moaned silently to herself. This was not the way she had planned it. How could she show Damon how much she loved him, how much she had missed him, if he overwhelmed her now? Struggling to her knees, she broke the kiss.

Holding her fingers against his lips, stopping him from again fastening his mouth on her, she whispered, "No. Let me."

"Feeling adventurous, my brave Christi?" Damon asked her softly.

Christiana just smiled as she ran her hands up

Damon's massive chest. A slow smile. A sensual smile. A smile full of promise. Damon watched her face as the smile transformed it. He let her push him back across the foot of the bed and prepared to suffer her ministrations.

Christiana leaned over him and placed her lips briefly on his. When he tried to wrest control of the kiss away from her, she pulled back, laughing deep in her throat. "Naughty, naughty," she chided. "You are in my power," she chanted. "You will move only when I tell you."

"I surrender to your greater power," Damon said, trying hard not to laugh, and failing.

"Hmm," Christiana said. "You're back to writing grade-B scripts again." She kissed and bit her way down Damon's strong neck, pausing at the wildly beating pulse she found in the hollow, soothing it with her tongue.

Damon groaned.

"But I forgive you," she said, magnanimously. Delicately she nipped her way up his collarbone, leaving a trail of fire in her wake.

Damon squirmed.

"Forgive me?"

"Of course. The superior power should always be forgiving of lesser being's foibles." She moved down his massive chest, tangling her fingers in the mat of hair that covered the bulging muscles. It lay in thick swirls around his flat, male nipples. With slow, deliberate movements, she touched him with her dainty tongue.

Damon gasped out loud.

Christiana played with the mat of hair, all the while

flicking her tongue over first one flat nipple then the other, gently biting the tiny nubs.

Damon arched his back.

"You're sure you're the superior power?" he gasped.

"Absolutely. Everyone knows that men only think they are superior because that's what women allow them to believe."

Christiana's hand trailed down to Damon's waist, where she tugged at the fastening of his pants.

"So you think I'm a lesser power?" Damon persisted, leading Christiana on as she pushed his pants down his legs.

"Yes." Her lips followed her hands, moving through the triangle of hair that grew low on his stomach, pointing the way to his throbbing sex.

Damon's lower body surged upward. Then, in one swift move, he turned and pulled Christiana under him. Taking her hand in his, he guided her to him.

"Lesser?" he teased.

"Much lesser," Christiana whispered.

"You're sure about that?" he asked, folding her fingers around him.

"Oh."

"Incomplete statement," Damon said, biting out the words. "The witness is instructed to give a full and complete statement."

"Not, not full," Christiana panted. "Empty. So empty."

"Shall I fill you, Christiana? My Christi, my love," Damon murmured as he hovered over her.

Christiana answered the only way she could. She guided him to her and thrust her hips upward to receive him as he filled her with his love.

* * *

Parker slammed the car door shut. Propping both hands against the top he stared at the front door of Christiana's house. His fingers drummed against the shiny metal as he told himself to calm down.

Drawing a deep breath, he tried. He knew he was very upset. *Upset, my ass*, he thought furiously. *I'm mad as hell!* He forced himself to take several more deep breaths before striding up the walk to the house.

He pressed savagely on the bell, waited perhaps five seconds, then pushed it again. When the door did not open immediately, he jabbed the button again and again. Finally, Peggy opened the door.

"Parker. Where's the fire? Don't just stand there. C'mon in."

"Peggy." Parker barely acknowledged her as he stomped through the door into the foyer. "Is Christiana home?"

"Yep. In the family room." She took his tan poplin windbreaker and hung it in the closet. "You know the way."

Parker stopped in the doorway to the family room, staring intently at Christiana. She looked the same as always, he thought. Then he swore to himself. *What did you expect, Lloyd? For her to change almost overnight into a flashy bimbo? Damon Law's brand on her forehead?* Taking another deep breath, he entered the room. "Hello, Christiana."

"Parker! So it was you leaning on my doorbell. What's wrong?"

"Wrong? Nothing. Why should there be? I just wanted to see you, that's all."

"Yeah," she laughed up at him. "How long has it been? Weeks! Suddenly you're so desperate to see me you can't even wait for Peggy to get to the door? Come on, Parker."

She patted the couch beside her. "Where've you been? I've missed you."

"Oh, here and there," he said, sitting where she indicated and draping a careless arm around her shoulders.

"You've been 'there,' maybe, but not 'here.' Who did you follow home this time, and just where did you go?"

"Remember the little Italian contessa?" Parker asked.

"Vaguely. Oh, Parker! Don't tell me you've been to Rome!"

"Okay," he laughed. "I won't tell you I've been to Rome."

"Parker, Parker," she said woefully. "When are you going to settle down?"

"Never, probably. But don't you start on me, lady. Not when I came to lecture *you*."

"You're here to fuss at me? Why? What have I done?"

"You don't know?" he drawled. "Now who's being obtuse?"

"Guess what? I'm going to Los Angeles Monday," she said brightly. Christiana did not think she had a snowball's chance of diverting Parker from his intention, but it was worth a try.

"Changing the subject won't work, Christiana, but I'll bite. Why are you going to L.A.?"

"Someone wants to buy my house!"

"The one in the canyon?" Parker asked, startled. "I didn't know you were thinking of selling."

"I wasn't. But they've made me a good offer."

"One you can't refuse, hey?"

"Something like that. I've decided it's time I let go of that part of my life."

"Does Damon Law have anything to do with this decision?" Parker asked skeptically. "And speaking of Damon Law, that reminds me why I'm here."

Christiana pulled one leg up under her and turned to face her friend. *Remember*, she told herself. *He cares about you.* "Why do I have the feeling I'm not going to enjoy this conversation?"

"Probably because you aren't," he snapped at her. "Dammit, Christiana! I leave the country for a couple of weeks, and what happens? You flip your lid, that's what!"

"Really, Parker. Flip my lid? You make me sound like a cigarette lighter!"

"Don't split hairs, Christi. And don't try to distract me. It won't work. You know very well what I mean."

"I assume," she said succinctly, "you are referring to my growing friendship with Damon Law?"

"No. I am not referring to your 'growing friendship' with Damon Law. I am referring to your growing *affair* with one of the more notorious womanizers of our time!"

"I always heard it takes one to know one," Christiana shot back.

"Dammit, Christiana . . ." Parker began, only to be interrupted by Christiana's firm voice.

"Calm down, Parker," she ordered. "I really don't see why you're so upset. After all, you, along with Peggy and Billy Joe, have been urging me for the last several months to get out and meet someone new. Those were your exact words, if I remember correctly. Now that I've done what you wanted, all of a sudden you're all singing a different tune." She threw her hands in the air. "There's just no pleasing the lot of you."

"Oh, for crying out loud, Christiana," he exploded. "What we wanted was for you to meet someone . . . someone . . ." He stammered to a stop.

"Someone like Johnny?" Christiana finished the sentence for him. "Forget it, Parker. I'm not looking for another Johnny. There isn't one." Christiana reached for Parker's hand. "Now tell me . . ." she said quietly. "Why don't you like Damon?"

"I didn't say that I don't like him. I do. He's a helluva fine fellow."

"Then I don't understand your objections."

"I'm not a woman," he said evasively.

"Obviously," she laughed. "But what has your gender to do with the discussion at hand?"

"It's because I'm not a woman that I can allow myself to be friends with Damon Law."

"Now, wait just a doggone minute," Christiana said. "Are you saying that it's dangerous for a woman to be friends with Damon?"

"Yes," Parker said, glad that Christiana had understood his oblique statement.

"That's the biggest crock of *bull* I've ever heard in my life!" she said in a very soft voice.

"Now, Christiana . . ." Parker said soothingly.

"Don't you 'now Christiana' me," she warned, preparing for battle.

"Damon, he . . ." Parker began, stuttering as he tried to find some way to say what he wanted without just coming right out with it. "Oh, hell!" He gave up searching for the right words. "He uses women, Christi. He's a user."

"Isn't everyone, one way or another? Aren't you?" she challenged.

"I suppose so," Parker admitted grudgingly. "But not like Damon Law. And unlike our friend Damon," he emphasized the word "friend" slightly, "I stick to women who know the score." He surged to his feet and paced up and down in front of her. "Christiana, honey," he pleaded, "I'm afraid he'll hurt you."

"I appreciate your concern, Parker, but isn't that my worry?" she said, her anger fading in the face of her friend's concern.

He pounced on her statement. "Are you worried? Are you afraid that he will hurt you?"

"Don't put words in my mouth. What I'm saying is, I'm a big girl now. I'm able to pick my own friends. I'm also able to judge how far I want to go in a relationship. Parker, what I'm saying is, this is my business and you're trespassing."

"Dammit," he said, stopping in front of her, "don't you think I know that?"

"Then why are you doing this?"

"Because I care about you." He touched her cheek gently. "You are the only person in this whole wide world who gives a tinker's damn about whether I live or die. I can't just sit idly by and let Damon Law wring you out and hang you up to dry without at least trying. Dammit, Christiana, I love you!"

"I know." Christiana stood, and, reaching up, planted a kiss on his cheek. "I love you too, Parker."

Parker put his arms around her and gave her a big hug.

"You had better have a damn good reason for putting your hands on my woman, Lloyd." A hard, cold voice split the air like the crack of a whip.

"Damon!" Christiana's face broke into a radiant smile. "I wasn't expecting you!"

"That's pretty obvious, Christi. Do you want to tell me what's going on here?"

Christiana's smile faded. *Uh oh*, she thought. *How much did he see and hear? Does he know that Parker was warning me away from him?* "Nothing of any importance, Damon," she finally said nervously. "I was just telling Parker that I'm going to Los Angeles next week."

Damon heard the slight quivering in Christiana's voice. He noticed also that when she tried to pull away from Parker he seemed reluctant to let her go. His face hardened into an implacable mask.

"Good-bye, Lloyd. Sorry you can't stay," Damon said, walking over and pulling Christiana away from him.

"Damon!" Christiana was aghast. "What do you think you are doing? Stop it this instant!"

"Lloyd knows what's going on," Damon said bluntly.

"Well, I don't! And in case either of you have forgotten, this is my house!"

"Calm down, Christi. Everything's under control."

The look of ownership Damon cast over Christiana as he tucked her protectively under his arm did not go unnoticed by Parker.

"That's the way of it, huh?" he asked Damon softly.

"You got it," Damon said quietly but with an underlying note of iron.

"Right, I'm gone." Parker stopped in the hall door and looked back at the couple standing in the middle of the room. A faint smile tugged at his mouth as he brought up his hand and tossed Damon a mocking salute. Then he left, grudgingly admitting to himself that he was leaving Christiana in good hands.

"Damon! Parker! Would someone please tell me what's going on here!" Christiana demanded.

"Nothing, Christi. Parker just decided he couldn't stay." Damon guided her back to the couch and sat down, pulling her into his lap.

"But . . ." she started to protest.

"Shut up, woman, and kiss me," Damon interrupted her.

Christiana did as he asked.

A few minutes later Damon set her away from him. Christiana, unwilling to leave him, slid her arms around his neck.

"Oh, no, Christi," Damon said, firmly pulling her hands down. "I want to talk, and we don't get much conversing done while we're touching each other."

"That, Mr. Law, is as much your fault as mine," she replied.

"I know, I know," he chuckled. "But my hands seem to have a mind of their own when they get anywhere near your delightful body."

"Flattery will get you everywhere," Christiana said, trying to snuggle next to him.

"Christiana . . ." Damon said threateningly.

"Okay, I'll be good." She scooted to the far corner of the couch. "What did you want to talk about that's more important than kissing me?"

"Talk about hitting below the belt!" Damon complained. "The way you put that, anything I say now will be wrong."

"Then look out, here I come," Christiana launched herself at him with such enthusiasm, Damon caught her close and kissed her. Which was exactly what she wanted in the first place.

Several minutes went by. Damon finally pulled away, and blinked at Christi. "Woman," he said plaintively, "I swear, I believe you could make me forget my name!"

"Could I?" Christiana asked with a wicked grin. "Let's try it again and see if I can."

"No." Damon fought her off, laughing as she tried to get past his defense. Standing up, he scooped her up in his arms and placed her firmly in her corner of the couch. "Now stay there," he ordered.

"Okay," Christiana sniffed, pretending to be insulted. "If that's what you want."

"Faker," he said, basking in the security of her feeling for him that allowed her to tease. "Christiana . . ." His tone was suddenly serious. "I'm going to ask you one more time. What's Parker to you?"

"He's my friend." Christiana heard the unspoken plea for reassurance in Damon's voice and responded in kind.

"A friend who loves you?" he asked skeptically.

"Like a brother," Christiana said, convinced she was right in her analysis of the situation.

Damon held his tongue. Christiana might love Parker like a sister loves a brother, but he was almost certain the feelings on Parker's side were stronger, more erotic, than brotherly love. But, since Parker had acknowledged Damon the winner in their little struggle, he decided he would let it go. After all, if Christiana had not picked up on Parker's deeper feeling for her, he really did not have anything to worry about. He reached for her almost absently, pulling her onto his lap.

Giving in to his growing desire, he kissed her thoroughly, moving his hand up her now-familiar curves, over her hip to her nipped-in waist. There he paused for a moment, feeling the satin smoothness of her skin.

Impatiently, Christiana wriggled, pressing her aching breast against his chest.

"Christiana . . ." he began, only to have her interrupt him breathlessly.

"What was the purpose of that interrogation?" she asked running her hands over his chest and up to cup his face lovingly.

"What was what?" Damon mumbled, his wandering hands reaching under her sweater to her swollen breasts to tug at the throbbing nipples.

"Nothing," Christiana replied, sinking into a swirl of passion. She was vaguely aware that Damon had left the couch and the family room behind and was carrying her up the stairs to her bedroom. "Ab-so-lute-ly nothing," she sighed.

The El Camino Hotel in Los Angeles had become a regular hangout. Christi had talked to lots of Johnny's old friends in the last few days. In addition to the musicians who roamed in and out of the hotel and bar, many of the movie people had discovered the picturesque hotel.

The dining room was filled with subdued noises: the sound of silver clinking against bone china; soft murmurs of quiet conversation; the discreet clink of a wine bottle against crystal.

Billy Joe put his knife and fork down, wiped his mouth with his napkin, shoved his plate away, and reached for his coffee. "That hit the spot. I was hungry." He sipped from the steaming cup. "You girls like to've worked me to death. Christiana, how did you and Johnny manage to collect so much stuff out here, anyway? I don't remember us being in L.A. that often. When did you have the time?"

"You call what you did work?" Peggy scoffed. "You spent all day wandering from the garage to the pool house and back to the garage again. I noticed you stayed away from the main house where the *real* work was going on." She looked pointedly at Billy Joe's plate, which had been scraped clean. "Are you sure you've had enough to eat? There are more crackers in the basket. Maybe the waiter would bring you some peanut butter?"

"Stuff it, Peggy," he said matter-of-factly. "You're just jealous because this isn't your cooking. Don't worry, babe. You're still the best cook I know. I was just so hungry after lugging all those boxes around for you girls these last two days, I could've eaten a steer. Hide and all."

"Brag, brag, brag," Peggy laughed.

"He has a point, Peggy," Christi said. "I didn't realize we'd left so many things out here. It's a good thing the buyer wants the furniture. No telling how long it would take to sell it off. Do you two think we will finish up here tomorrow?"

"Yeah," Billy Joe said. "Tomorrow should wrap things up. Hey, wasn't it something, that real estate lady coming up with a buyer?"

"Especially with the market the way it's been lately," Peggy said, pushing aside her unfinished dinner. "I don't know about you, Christi, but I'm just too tired to eat."

"Are you sure you're not just making an excuse not to eat anyone else's cooking than your own?" Billy Joe teased.

"I don't doubt she's tired," Christiana said. "You should be, too. You two have done all the work this last couple of days. All I did was sit around, mooning over the past."

"Or yearning for the future, perhaps?" Peggy asked, a smile in her voice.

"Perhaps." Christiana's soft voice did not presage a display of temper these day. It usually meant she was thinking about Damon.

"But I'm tired, too, Peggy. I'll be glad for tomorrow to come and go. That means we'll be finished going through the house, and can turn it over to the realtor."

"Frankly, I'm really surprised she found a buyer," Billy Joe persisted. "It's strange. Houses are sitting empty all over the place since the bottom fell out of the market."

"I'm surprised, too," Christiana said. "The last thing I expected when I answered the phone last Friday was an offer for the house."

"Do you know who's buying the house, Christi?" Billy Joe asked.

"No. The realtor just said an actress."

"Were you thinking about selling," Peggy asked, "or did this offer decide things?"

"No. I hadn't thought about selling until she called. But it's time for me to cut loose from this place. I don't even know why I was holding on to it. I'll never come back here to live." Christiana drank the last of her coffee and stood up. "If you're through eating, Billy Joe, I want to get upstairs so I'll be there for Damon's call."

TEN

Upstairs in the suite, Christiana moved about her room, slowly preparing for the night. She missed Damon with an ache that threatened to consume her.

To make matters worse, she was surrounded with strange sounds. Los Angeles was an alien place for her now. She heard the sound from the TV blare out in the living room, then die down as the volume was lowered. Billy Joe must have turned it on to listen to the news. She missed the familiar voices of the newscasters back in Houston.

Going into the bathroom, she showered and was brushing her teeth when she thought she heard the phone ringing. Excited, as always, at the prospect of talking to Damon, she began to hurry. A minute later Peggy called to her through the closed door.

"Speed it up in there, Chris. Damon's on the phone."

"I'll be right out." Christiana quickly finished brushing her teeth. Pulling her nightgown over her still-

157

slightly-damp body, she hurried into the bedroom and picked up the phone beside her bed.

"Hi, Christi." Damon's voice floated out of the earpiece before she had a chance to get it to her ear.

"Hi yourself. You're early tonight." Christiana lay back against the pillows, her left hand holding the phone, her right hand playing with the coiling wire that trailed across her satin-clad breasts.

"I've been calling every half hour since six o'clock. Where have you *been*?" he asked plaintively.

"In the dining room, pushing what was probably a perfectly good dinner around on my plate."

"Tired, love?" His voice was tender. "You don't have to work so hard. Slow down, take another day or two. Just because you told the realtor you would have all your possessions out of the house by tomorrow doesn't mean you have to kill yourself doing it."

"I know. I just want to get it over and done with. I'm lonesome!" she blurted, then clapped her hand over her mouth. The one thing she did not want to do was give Damon the idea that she was trying to pin him down.

In all the weeks she and Damon had been together, neither one of them had verbalized their feeling for the other. True, Damon called her "love" all the time, and "my love" when they were making love, but that didn't count.

"I know, Christi. I'm lonesome, too. Hey," he laughed, "remember the old musical *Seven Brides for Seven Brothers*?"

"Yes."

"Remember the 'Lonesome Polecat' sequence?"

"Yes." Christiana was grinning now.

"Well, I'm like that 'mean ole hound dawg, bayin' at the moon,' down here all by myself."

Christiana laughed. "I'm lonesome, but not quite *that* lonesome!"

"Of course not. You've got Peggy and Billy Joe. All I've got for company is an assistant producer who, when he isn't popping antacid pills, is screaming about money, and a sour-faced director who hates every site I've chosen."

"You could always go out to Parker's. I'm sure there's some action there," she suggested, roguish laughter coloring her voice.

"Christi . . ." Damon said heavily, "I wouldn't touch that one with a ten-foot pole."

"Getting smart in your old age, Law?" she queried sweetly.

"I just want to live to see my old age," he shot back.

"Who are you more afraid of, Damon," Christiana laughed, "Parker? Or yourself?"

"Neither, Christi. It's you who strikes terror in my heart. I hate to think of the consequences if you even hear of me sniffing around another woman."

"Now I know you're getting smart," she said happily. Damon had just told her, in a roundabout way, that he was being faithful to her.

"Did your realtor tell you how much she was able to get for your house?" Damon asked.

"Yes." Christiana named the amount. "I think, all things considered, it's a good price."

"It's a damn good price. Keep that lady's card. If I ever have to sell any of my California property, I want her to handle it. Say . . ." he asked thoughtfully, "you wouldn't be interested in investing this sudden windfall in a sure-fire, multimillion-dollar box-office smash, would you?''

"I might," Christiana said slowly. What was Damon asking her? To invest the proceeds from the sale of the house in his next film? Or to expand their relationship? "Would my investment help?"

"It sure would. And once all the business is taken care of, most of my contribution is over. Oh, I'll still have to be available for conferences. There's a multitude of things that go wrong, but, essentially, the hard work is done. I'd have more time to spend with you," he said slyly. "Maybe we could even get back down to Surf Side—and stay longer this time."

"You sure know how to push the right buttons, Mr. Law," she said. "I'll tell you what. When I get home, I'll have a long talk with my accountant. As things stand now, I can't think of any reason why I shouldn't invest in your production. As far as I know, everything you've had anything to do with has made money."

"I can almost guarantee it, love. But what's more important is that we will be partners. Of course, you do realize that partners have to spend lots and lots of time with each other—taking care of business."

"Of course."

"I can think of some very nice 'business' that I'd like to be taking care of right now," Damon said, his voice dropping sexily.

"Me, too."

"The only problem is, I'm miles away from my 'business,' " he said sadly.

"Me, too."

"I sure do miss my 'business.' " His voice was forlorn, as if he'd lost his last friend.

"Me, too."

"Christiana, there's an echo on this phone!" Damon laughed. "I keep hearing someone saying, 'me, too.' "

"Me, too," Christiana said, dissolving into laughter. "Me, too."

"Oh, Christi, I do miss you." Damon talked on, telling Christiana just how much he missed her, and just exactly what he would like to be doing with her right now.

They talked for the better part of two hours. As she was getting ready to say good-bye, Christiana said, "Hey. If we keep running up these huge phone bills, maybe I'd better think about investing in AT&T."

"No way, Christi. If you're not back here in a couple more days, I'm dropping everything and coming out there. Being a martyr is not my thing, and I'm definitely not cut out to be a long-distance lover."

"I don't think you'll have to do anything so drastic, Damon. We should wrap everything up tomorrow. If not then, the next day for sure."

"All right! On that happy note, I'll say good night, Christi. I miss you." The last words faded away as Damon hung up.

"Good night, my love," Christiana whispered to the silent receiver. She sat for a long time after Damon broke the connection, holding the phone nestled against her breast.

"I wish he had said, 'I love you,' " she whispered longingly. "Oh, no, I don't," she argued, sitting up abruptly and putting the receiver back in its cradle. "Not really. Not on the phone. I want to be in his arms when he tells me he loves me—if he ever does!"

With these conflicting thoughts, she turned down the covers and crawled into bed.

At five-thirty the next afternoon, Billy Joe put the

last box into the rented pickup. "That's it," he said, breathing a sigh of relief. "We're through."

"Thank goodness," Christiana said, echoing his sigh. She had finished her part of the packing earlier in the afternoon, deciding what to keep and what to send to Goodwill.

For the last half hour, she had been tucked out of the way, leaving Peggy and Billy Joe free to move around without worrying about bumping into her. She was sitting beside the empty pool in an old-fashioned porch swing.

Memories. The whole place brought back memories. Even the swing she was sitting in. Johnny had bought it from a little old man who sold the handmade swings from the back of his garage. He had been so excited when he brought it home. When she pointed out that they did not have a screened porch to hang it on, his face fell. Then he thought of putting it beside the pool.

A lot of mishaps and laughter had resulted, but eventually the poles were standing upright and the crossbar was in place. When they hung the swing, Johnny had christened it with half a bottle of vintage champagne.

The party that had evolved that day was one of her most cherished memories. Before the afternoon had faded into evening, all of Johnny's band, plus many of the studio musicians had wandered by. How had the word spread? Christiana never knew. Musicians had a telegraph that rivaled Western Union in its heyday. They came to razz, but stayed to help, then to party.

Who brought out the first guitar? She couldn't remember that, either, but it hadn't been long before they were doing what musicians like best—jamming. The food had been simple, hot dogs and hamburgers, but it had been fun! No one drank too much beer. No one became obnoxious. No one started a fight. They just sat around, picking and singing and having a good time.

There had been music, talk, and laughter—the same ingredients that went into making up one of Parker's parties. But the two parties were as different as night and day.

Thinking of Parker and his parties just naturally brought Christiana's thoughts around to Damon. She would be home tomorrow. And tomorrow she would be with him, feel his strong arms around her, lose herself in his kiss.

"That's the last of them." Billy Joe's voice broke into her thoughts. He sank down into a chair beside Christiana. "Everything is loaded and tied down."

He swept his hat off, at the same time wiping his sweaty forehead with his shirtsleeve. He pulled the brim down low over his eyes, hiding the hunger in his gaze as he watched Peggy walking smoothly toward them.

"Thank goodness," Christiana sighed. "Now we can go home."

"Yeah," Peggy said, sitting beside her. "I'm getting homesick. Say, Christi. Are you sure you don't want this furniture? It's nice stuff. And some of the rugs are really beautiful."

"Peggy . . ." Billy Joe rummaged around in the cooler at his feet and came up with a beer. "If you don't hush, I just might be forced to tape your mouth shut." He turned the can up and took a long swallow. "You can think of the damnedest things."

"You and what army?" Peggy snapped.

"You know, Billy Joe," Christi said, popping the top on the cola Peggy handed her, "I just might be forced to help you. If Peggy keeps on, we won't be going home tomorrow."

"Okay! Okay! I'm just trying to help."

"Sure you are," Christiana teased, laughing with Billy Joe when Peggy became flustered. "Are you two sure we have everything?" she asked. "Did you check the garden shed?"

"You asked me that already," Billy Joe complained.

Peggy stood and turned toward the kitchen door. "If you're gonna start whining, Billy Joe, I'm splitting. I'll be in the kitchen, Christi."

A minute later, Billy Joe, deciding he'd better mend his fences with Peggy, said, "Holler if you need me, Chris," and left.

Thoughtfully, Christiana finished her soda. It was sad to think that when she climbed into the truck and left, she would never enter this house again.

Standing up, she felt her way carefully and went into the house. Passing Billy Joe talking earnestly to Peggy at the kitchen table, she said, "I'll be back shortly. I'm going through the house."

"One last time?" Peggy asked knowingly.

"You know me so well, Peggy," Christiana laughed self-consciously. "Yes. One last time. To say goodbye."

That evening Christiana was once again in the hotel dining room, listening to the muted sounds around her. This time she was alone, enjoying a last cup of coffee.

Peggy and Billy Joe were in the bar, having a last-minute reunion with some old friends. They had tried to get her to come with them, but she shooed them away. The memories that just being in Los Angeles brought to mind, combined with actually selling the house in the canyon, had left her feeling a little melancholy.

Her last stroll through the house had been bittersweet. The finality of what she was doing, selling this part of her life with Johnny, brought on a feeling of panic. It had almost caused her to call the realtor and back out of her agreement.

Each room, each item, brought back memories. Most were happy, but some were sad. How had she ever gathered the courage to face them?

Sitting here now, drinking her coffee, she realized that she was slightly punch drunk. She had been hit from so many sides, by so many different emotions, that she was still reeling from the impact.

If it hadn't been for Damon . . .

Christiana shook her head. She couldn't blame her actions on Damon. True, he had probably speeded things up by forcing her to get out more. If he had not entered her life, stirring up her sedentary pace, she might never have reached the point she was at today.

But Damon was in her life. He was real and warm and alive. And she loved him. That, perhaps, was the greatest single thing that had allowed her to put aside her past and concentrate on the future.

Enough. Christiana carefully placed her cup on its saucer. She wanted to talk to Damon. She would call him tonight, rather than wait for him to call her. She was about to signal the waiter and ask him to fetch Billy Joe from the bar when she heard, "Damon Law?"

The voice, a woman's, came from the table behind her. Curious, without stopping to think that eavesdroppers never hear anything good, Christiana dropped her hand into her lap and listened.

"Really, darling," the voice continued, "are you

sure this is not all wishful thinking on your part? Damon Law has never been known to go back to a woman he has dropped. Although," the voice became speculative, "if looks are what it takes to get him to make the rounds twice, you just might get him. I'd kill for your hair and eyes. Flame-red and emerald-green. And they're natural!" she said. "Not a drop of dye or a contact lens! Some people get all the luck!"

A light, musical voice answered this strange combination of praise and envy. "In the first place, Ginger, I did the discarding, not Damon. And, because of that, I'm going to be the one who gets him back. Permanently."

"Lissa! Do you really think so? Tell me all about it!" the woman called Ginger gushed. "That picture in Sunday's paper of Damon kissing you good-bye in the Atlanta airport was steamy. I swear, my bones just melted when I saw it. But," she paused, biting off the word as if she had just thought of something important, "what about Christiana Smith? The last I heard, Damon was giving her the bum's rush down in Houston."

"Bum's rush is right," Lissa said in her musical voice. Christiana's accurate hearing picked up an underlying trace of scorn.

"Oh? What do you mean by that?" Ginger's voice went higher with each word as she sensed a juicy bit of gossip.

"It's obvious to anyone who knows Damon's reputation as a producer. He always insists on absolute accuracy in his films," Lissa said.

"But of course! That's what almost got you thrown out of that picture you made for him."

"Yes, well, that's neither here nor there." Lissa waved aside an unpleasant memory. "What I'm getting at is Damon's newest picture. It's all about . . . a blind woman!" Triumphant satisfaction oozed from every word.

"Sooo," Ginger hissed. " 'Lady Christiana' is nothing to Damon Law but research."

"Yes!" Lissa laughed. "Isn't it delightful? While she stays home in Houston, I'm keeping Damon company in Atlanta! That way, I get Damon, and Damon gets his research!"

"And what does the little widow get?"

"Exactly what she deserves," Lissa said carelessly.

"Lissa Andrews, you are a sly, cunning devil of a woman," Ginger said admiringly. "Don't forget, now," the sounds of chairs being pushed back intruded, "send me an invitation to the wedding!"

"Don't worry, darling. Your name will head the list!" Their voices faded as they walked away from the table.

For a moment—for one blessed, beautiful moment— Christiana did not comprehend what she had heard. Then the words bouncing around in her head sorted themselves out and she understood.

The sounds of the diners, the soft voices of the waiters, even the music from the trio discreetly hidden in a corner, all faded away. All she was conscious of was pain. Agonizing, suffocating pain, pain so intense she could not move, could barely even breath. *Surely*, she thought wildly, *surely now I will die*.

Then, like a large wave washing over the shore, feeling returned to her numb body. A low, gasping moan escaped her lips as she leaned over, clutching her stomach with her crossed arms.

The hollow pain centered in her midsection began to grow. Her ears rang with the rush of blood, spurred on by surging adrenaline. Her throat felt thick, the muscles rigid and boardlike. Her tongue seemed to cleave stiffly to the roof of her mouth. A heavy pressure settled in her chest, clutching at her heart and lungs. She wanted to collapse in a heap on the table and scream her hurt and betrayal.

With a slight shudder, she remembered she was in a public place. Taking a deep breath, she sat up straight, squared her shoulders, and unconsciously lifted her chin. When Peggy came for her a few minutes later, she was able to walk out of the dining room just as though everything was right with her world. Billy Joe joined them while they waited for the elevator, and he and Peggy talked softly about old times and old friends. Christiana did not hear them. She did not hear any of the noises in the busy lobby. Her thoughts were turned inward, to that place deep in her mind where she, and only she, could go.

She roused out of her self-induced stupor enough to wonder irritably why the elevator was so slow. Then the doors swished open and they were on their way.

Entering the suite, she went directly into her room, closing and locking the door. Carefully, she removed her shoes and stretched out on the bed, her hands folded neatly on her stomach. She tried to keep her mind blank, but, slowly, then faster and faster, the echoing voices seeped past her mental barrier.

She loved, and her love saw her as an object of research. He had dissected her, and observed her to see what made her tick. This was what she had been reduced to. Something to be examined, then tossed away.

Used.

The warmth, the laughter, the friendship, the loving—everything was false. She felt dirty, inside and out. Violated. Betrayed.

She laughed. A short, hysterical, barking sound. She should have known, she thought, clapping her hand over her mouth. Oh, God! She should have known!

She forced back the flood of feelings this small break in her iron control threatened. She couldn't afford to let even one small memory creep past her defenses. If she did, she was surely lost.

Instinctively she knew she could survive only if she did not think of Damon. Therefore, she would not think of him. For all practical purposes he must cease to exist for her. She had to wipe out the last few weeks. Erase them from her life as if they had never been.

Damon Law had never kissed her. He had never pursued her relentlessly, gently forcing her to get out, go places, and do things on her own. He had never asked her to spend those glorious days at Surf Side with him.

He had never loved her.

Tears streamed silently down Christiana's face as she mourned. She mourned the loss of dreams, the loss of love, the loss of innocence. Never again, she vowed. Never again would she be so vulnerable. Twice she had loved, and twice she had lost her love through no fault of her own. Never again would she be so misguided as to seek love. She could not survive if she had to go through this loss one more time. She knew now that love was not for her.

Slowly, second by second, thought by thought, she began to build back up the protective wall Damon had torn down. She needed it. Like a wounded animal, she had to hide away.

The ringing of the phone penetrated her defenses only because subconsciously she had been listening for it.

She tensed, knowing that it was Damon who was calling. When Peggy knocked on her door, she was ready.

"Hey, Christi. It's Damon—as if you didn't know." Peggy, already turning back into the living room, was jerked to a stop by Christiana's reply.

"What did you say?" she asked, not believing her own ears.

"You heard me."

"You're sure?"

"Yes!"

"Okay. If you say so . . . Damon?" Peggy said, her puzzlement reflected in her voice, "Chris says she doesn't want to talk to you. I guess she's too tired." Peggy made a lame excuse for Christiana's behavior.

"Tired?" Damon couldn't believe what he was hearing. "What the hell do you mean, 'too tired?' What's happened, Peggy?"

"Beats me," Peggy shrugged. "I think she's just a little burned out, you know?"

"Oh," Damon said, hurting for Christiana. Dammit! If only he could have gone with her! Damn these idiots he was working with for dragging their heels at every little thing. "It's been rough on her, hasn't it, Peggy?"

"Yeah. But not as rough as it would have been if she hadn't had you waiting for her."

"Oh, well," Damon laughed self-consciously. "I should be there with her. Tell her to get a good night's sleep, and I'll see her tomorrow."

"Will do. Later, Damon."

"Good night, Peggy."

Back at The Woodlands Inn, Damon looked long and hard at the telephone he had just replaced on the counter. He had carried it over to the easy chair, preparing to settle in and be comfortable while having a long talk with Christiana. Now, for the first time since he had met her at Parker's, she was refusing to talk to him.

Too tired, my ass! he thought savagely. Something was wrong. He felt it on a gut level. This wasn't like that day just a few short weeks ago, when she refused his call. That had been more like a game. This . . . this had a feeling of finality about it.

Slamming his fist into his palm, he turned to pace the floor. Why did she have to be all the way across the country? He would have to wait, and he hated waiting. Forcing himself to be calm, he rationalized that he could wait until tomorrow to see her. But he wanted to be with her now, take her in his arms and soothe away her fears.

Fears? Why should she be afraid? Was it because he had rashly suggested she invest in his film? Did she think that all he was after was her money? Damn! He shouldn't have said anything to her about his idea until she got back. But he had been so excited about the prospect of them working together, he had thrown caution to the wind.

Now, he was reaping the results of his impatience. Well, he thought resignedly, he would sort it out when Christiana came home.

Christiana lay tense and silent on her bed. Even though she had decided to erase Damon from her life, her thoughts would not be controlled. Like a flash sequence in an avant garde movie, her mind insisted on playing back the times she had spent with Damon.

Bits and pieces floated past her mind's eye. Sounds,

smells, laughter, touching and being touched, kissing and being kissed, loving and being loved.

Stop it! she commanded herself. *This way lies insanity!*

But, in spite of her determination, she remembered. And, remembering, writhed in shame.

This is what you get, Christiana Smith, she thought wildly, *for thinking that Damon Law would ever be interested in someone like you. This is what you get for thinking you could make him love you. Idiot. Don't you know you can't force someone to love you?*

What you shared with Damon, in spite of your hopes, was passion, lust. Not love. Love was what you had with Johnny. Johnny's gone, and so is love.

Suddenly, she was angry at Johnny for going away and leaving her, alone and unloved. Didn't he know he was the reason for her existence? Didn't he know that without him she was lost? What was she, really, without him? Just an ordinary woman with no particular talents or beauty. And in addition, she was blind! What man would want her?

She had been right, that long-ago evening at Parker's. The only thing she represented to Damon Law was challenge. She hadn't thrown herself at his feet so he set out to conquer her.

With her willing, eager help, he knocked down her defenses. His conquest was so quick and so thorough she must have ceased to be a challenge to him within a couple of weeks—by the time he made his first trip to Atlanta.

Oh, God! She felt sick! What a fool she had been. What a complete and utter fool!

And what a fool she still was. For, in spite of it all, she loved him.

If only he had not made that trip to Atlanta! If only she had not heard Lissa Andrews gloating to Ginger! If only Damon would walk through her door right now and tell her it was all a dreadful mistake. If only . . .

A mistake! Was it? Could it be possible? Could it all be a mistake? The evidence, damning as it was, was only hearsay.

Suppose it was all wishful thinking on Lissa's part? Suppose she was just bragging to that Ginger person?

Was she, Christiana, making the classic mistake of condemning Damon without a hearing? Would he have an explanation? Was he actually innocent of the heartless actions described by the catty woman?

She had to know. She could not live with herself if she made such an absurd blunder. Tomorrow she would talk to Damon. Tomorrow, when she was home again. When she could talk to Damon in person, not over the impersonal long-distance wires. She would ask him about Lissa Andrews and Atlanta. And about the movie, whose heroine was a blind woman.

Damon stood by the gate, waiting for Christiana. He waited impatiently for the crowd of arriving passengers to thin out. He knew Billy Joe and Peggy would not bring Christiana from the plane until everyone else had left. Restlessly, he paced back and forth.

At last! There they were, coming down the jetway. His eyes searched Christiana's face as she walked toward him. She looked tired and drawn, dammit. What did she do to herself in L.A.?

"Hello, Christi." With an effort he restrained himself from pulling her violently to him and smothering her with kisses. Instead, he held her face tenderly between his hands and bent to kiss her. "Miss me?"

He felt her stiffen when he touched her. As his lips lightly brushed hers, she flinched slightly and pulled away.

What was wrong?

ELEVEN

Prudently, he didn't press. "Come on, love," he said gently. "I'll take you home."

Christiana hesitated, not sure she wanted to be alone with Damon. *Not yet*, her tired mind clamored. *I can't handle this. I'm not ready! Idiot*, she chided herself, *you'll never be ready for this*.

"Yeah, Christiana," Billy Joe spoke up. "You go ahead with Damon. I'm going to take Peggy to her folks for a while."

That did it. There was no way she could insist on Billy Joe taking her home now. With a deep, fortifying breath, she turned to Damon and said, "Let's go."

The trip up the toll road into Montgomery County was fraught with tension. Damon tried. He really tried to keep the conversational ball going, but Christiana kept dropping it.

"How was your flight?" he asked jovially in the elevator to the parking garage.

"Okay," she said shortly. Christi was tense and nervous. She could barely force the single word through her tightened vocal cords. How did one go about asking one's lover if he was really her lover?

Damon, already worried by Christi's refusal to talk to him on the phone last night, read dismissal in the choked-off word. He was frightened that Christi was going to tell him to go away. He, Damon Law, who had carelessly severed numerous relationships, was terrified at the prospect of being sent away by a woman.

"Did you get the house turned over to the realtor?"

"Yes."

To Damon's sensitive ears her tone was flat, bored. He raked his fingers through his hair again as he glanced at the silent woman beside him. He wanted to stop the car, grab her, and shake some sense into her. He had to know what caused this drastic change in the loving woman who had left him so reluctantly a few days ago. Exerting all his strength of will, he forced himself to be patient. They were at the junction of the toll road and the freeway before he tried again. "Are you glad to be home?" he asked, expecting another monotone answer.

"I don't know."

Damon inserted the Vette into the freeway traffic before the words registered.

"What do you mean, you don't know?" His stomach muscles clenched as a little thrill of fear raced through him. She *was* going to tell him to get lost. She couldn't, he wouldn't! He'd fight for her.

"I have to ask you a question," she blurted.

This was it. His patience was paying off. Now he would find out what was wrong. Relief that she was talking to him drowned out the questions in his mind. Questions like, why was he so worried? Why didn't he just walk away from her, instead of waiting on her to end it? And why was he so determined to hold on to this woman?

"Okay, shoot."

"Well . . ." she hedged, "it's actually two questions."

"One, two, a hundred," he said shortly, "it doesn't matter. What do you want to know?"

"Damon?" her voice was hesitant.

"What, Christi?" The question was a weary sigh.

"Will you tell me the truth?"

"I've never lied to you, Christiana." What was it? What had happened to upset her?

"Yes. Well. Are you making a film about a blind woman?" she asked, all in a rush.

"Christiana . . ." he broke off, startled. *My God! Is that what this was all about? Who told her? When? How?*

"Just answer yes or no, please," she said firmly.

"Yes," he said grimly.

"You are?" she asked in a small voice. That wasn't what he was supposed to say! Where was the indignant denial, the reassurance she had hoped to hear?

"Yes!"

"Oh."

Christiana wrestled with, and finally accepted the fact, that Damon was heartlessly using her.

"That's one," Damon said as he steered the car onto The Woodlands Parkway overpass.

"What?" she said distractedly.

"That's one question. You said you had two," he reminded her.

"Oh, that's right. I have another question, don't I?"

She twisted her fingers in her lap until they were

bloodless. Damon reached over and placed his hand on hers, silently telling her that it was all right.

But it wasn't all right. She had a horrible premonition that nothing would ever be right again. Did she really want to ask her other question? No. Did she have any choice? Again, no.

They had reached her driveway when she took a deep breath and blurted, "Did-you-kiss-Lissa-Andrews-at-the-airport-in-Atlanta?"

"Christi, for God's sake!" Damon exploded. "This has gone far enough! Who's been talking to you?" He turned into her driveway and hit the brakes, throwing her against the seat belt.

"Did you?" she insisted.

"Christiana, you don't understand."

"Yes or no?" she persisted, interrupting him.

"Yes, dammit!"

"Thank you," she said with quiet dignity. Opening the door, she got out and stood beside the car. "You needn't get out."

"Don't be more of an ass than you can help, Christi," he said, his anger growing by leaps and bounds. Slamming his door shut and stomping around the front of the car, he took her arm.

"Please don't touch me," she said, her voice cold and distant.

"Christiana, I'm warning you."

"And I'm warning you!" she cried, turning on him furiously. "Leave me alone! Do you understand me?" she shouted. "Leave me alone."

Christiana found the walkway and stalked to her front door. Leaning her head against the cool wood, she said wearily, "Just go away, Damon." Her throat was tight with unshed tears and she had to force the words out. "Go away and don't come back."

"Christiana, love, if you'd just let me explain," he said, trying to hold on to his fast-dwindling patience.

Christiana jerked open the door and ran inside. The door slammed, and Damon found himself talking to solid wood. Furious at having the door slammed shut in his face, he twisted the knob, but Christiana had thrown the dead bolt.

His growing anger reached the boiling point and erupted. He pounded his fist on the door once, shaking the solid oak in its frame. A howl of anger, fear, and frustration escaped him and he yelled, "To hell with it. To hell with the whole damn thing!"

Spinning on his heel, he strode angrily down the walk to his car. The engine in his beloved Vette raced as his foot pumped the accelerator. The sound of metal grinding against metal shrieked in the quiet afternoon as he shifted into reverse. Tires squelled—and he roared away, running from his pain.

Some time later the red haze before his eyes began to clear. Inhaling deeply, he got a firm grip on his runaway emotions. The crisp, sharp odor of the sea stung his nostrils. Looking around, he was surprised to find himself in Surf Side. Turning onto the oyster-shell drive to his house a few minutes later, he cut the engine and sat, staring at the place where they had first made love.

Breathing deeply of the pungent salt air, he willed his mind to go blank. Then, carefully and deliberately, he reviewed everything that had transpired between him and Christiana from the time they left Intercontinental Airport until he peeled out of her driveway.

Stubborn, hardheaded woman, he thought as he remembered their last angrily shouted words. He gripped the steering wheel until his knuckles were white. God *damn* a woman who wouldn't listen . . . wouldn't let him explain . . .!

The little voice in the back of his head—the one he had been conveniently ignoring since he met Christiana—was asking him what the hell he was doing, trying to explain his actions to a woman?

He continued to ignore the cynical voice. This wasn't just any woman, for God's sake! This was Christiana! Besides, he hadn't behaved like his old self at any time since he met her—why should he start now?

Hunching over, he rested his folded arms on the steering wheel as he wondered which one of his enemies had gotten to Christiana.

Yes, he nodded his head, the information had been fed to her deliberately. He had been in the dog-eat-dog world of Hollywood too long to believe otherwise.

Bits and pieces of their argument continued to float around in his head. He let out a self-derisive snort as he remembered his own childish display of temper. *My God!* he thought incredulously, *did I really call my sweet Christiana an ass?*

Shaking his head at his stupidity, he thought he might possibly get her to forgive him. Somewhere around the year 2000!

Starting the car, he backed out of the drive and turned toward Houston. There was nothing else to do. He would have to go back and eat crow—after prudently giving Christiana enough time to cool off!

Christiana wore herself out crying. She was crying when she slammed the front door in Damon's face, and she cried the rest of that evening and into the night. Finally, when the grandfather clock in the living room downstairs struck four o'clock, she fell into an exhausted, fitful slumber.

When she came down to breakfast the next morning, Peggy, seeing her red, swollen eyes, was startled into asking what was wrong.

"Nothing," Christiana said sulkily, "that never hearing from Damon Law again won't cure!"

"I knew it," Billy Joe muttered. "I knew I was going to have to flatten that dude before it was all over."

"You'll do no such thing, Billy Joe Chambers!" Christiana ordered sharply. "The only thing I want, from any of you, and this includes Parker, is for you to keep him away from me."

"That's no way to solve a problem, Christi," Peggy warned, her gum snapping furiously. "You can't run away from this. It'll go with you, wherever you go."

"Peggy . . ." Christiana sighed heavily. "Believe me when I tell you this is one problem that is better left unsolved."

"Well, all I got to say is, if that dude comes around here, he's in for the surprise of his life," Billy Joe said darkly.

"Billy Joe," Christiana said warningly.

"Oh, don't worry about him, Chris. He's all bark and no bite. He'll do as you say, won't you, sport?" Peggy demanded of the defiant man.

"Maybe." Billy Joe did not want to give in.

"Please, Billy Joe. I don't want any trouble. I don't think I could handle it right now," Christiana pleaded.

"Well, okay," he agreed doubtfully, "if you're sure that's the way you want it."

"I'm sure," Christiana said. "Believe me. I only want to write *finis* to this whole thing and get on with my life." She laughed, a brittle little laugh that tore at her listeners' hearts. "Now that I know I can do more than just sit in this house, I have things to do, places to go, and people to meet!"

Christiana made up her mind she wouldn't cry anymore over Damon Law. After all, wasn't this just what she had expected? She knew she was taking a chance with him, but she had gambled that the strength of her love would break through the wall he had built around his heart. She had gambled and lost. She would be thankful for the time she had with him and get on with her life.

But a hundred times a day she relived a memory. In desperation she rehashed all the reasons she had given herself for not getting involved with him in the first place. She made herself remember how embarrassed she was, that first night at Parker's, when Damon had told her specifically what she had to offer him. With a fresh jab of pain, she realized he'd never told her what he had to offer her.

She recalled his arrogance, and, yes, his chauvinism. She remembered all the things that she had ignored during their relationship that told her, loud and clear, that Damon was not interested in anything permanent. He was a playboy. Playboys did not make commitments. She tried, she really tried, to put the interlude behind her—to drive Damon Law from her head. But she could not.

She would hear Peggy on the phone, telling Damon that no, Christiana would not talk to him—and remember the day when he called every few minutes, driving Peggy crazy with his persistence. And again, after

Damon pounded on the door until he was turned away by a belligerent Billy Joe, she remembered with painful clarity the morning she decided not to see him again.

No, she could not forget Damon Law. Circumstances, and Damon's stubborn determination not to take no for an answer, would not let her.

The next several days were an emotional rollercoaster ride. Her life had become a series of highs and lows. The highs were the infrequent times she was able to keep Damon Law out of her thoughts. The lows occurred when he called, or worse, came to the house, bringing all the memories, with their attendant pain and anguish, back into focus.

She did not follow through on her boast to Peggy and Billy Joe that she would take advantage of her newly found confidence and continue getting out and doing things. She tried once, but missed Damon so much, and was so totally miserable, that Billy Joe himself called the shopping trip off and took her home. She began spending time, as much as the unstable Texas weather allowed, in the hammock in the backyard. There, she was able to drift, unthinking, and consequently, unfeeling and unhurt. She was living in her memories, the way she had after Johnny died. She was reverting, withdrawing into herself, becoming a shell of the vibrant, laughing woman she had become in Damon's company.

Parker stood at the window, staring out at the listless woman in the hammock. He turned back with an oath into the room. Two remorseful figures sat stiffly on the sofa before him. If the situation had not been so desperate, he would have laughed. Their expressions were almost as glum as Christiana's.

"What the hell did you two let happen while I was gone?" he demanded, pacing the floor. He made a quick turn around the room, spinning on his heels to confront his listeners.

"What d'ya mean, what did we *let* happen?" Billy Joe was looking for an argument. He sprang from the couch to stand in front of Parker's face. "Listen you. In order to stop something from happening, you have to know it's gonna happen in the first place. Peggy and me, we ain't got the foggiest notion what this is all about." He waved his arm toward the backyard and Christiana lying so quietly in the hammock.

"Yeah, Parker. We don't know what happened," Peggy said. The barely concealed hostility between Parker and Billy Joe was upsetting her. She didn't need these two grown men fighting like little boys. She had all she could handle coping with Christi. She didn't know what she would do if they came to blows. Scream, probably.

"Okay," Parker sighed, sitting in Christiana's favorite overstuffed chair. He ran his hand down over his face and around, massaging the back of his neck. God, he was tired. Houston to New York, to Ireland, to Paris to Rome—with a quick trip to Tel Aviv just for fun—then home again in less than ten days had exhausted him. Maybe it was time for him to think about retiring. "Let's go over it one more time. She was all right until you got home from L.A.?"

"Yeah," Billy Joe said.

"No," Peggy said at the same time.

"What do you mean, 'no,' Peggy?" Parker asked, alert once more. Peggy knew something. He was sure of it. They just had to be patient and let her get to it in her own time and in her own way.

"I didn't think too much of it at the time. Well, I did, but . . ." Her voice trailed off as she remembered the series of events that took place that evening.

"When, Peggy? What?" Billy Joe broke in impatiently.

"Quiet, Billy Joe. Let her talk," Parker said. He knew that something traumatic had happened to Christiana, something so unthinkable that she had crawled back into her shell—the shell they had all worked so hard to pry her from after Johnny's death.

"We were through at the house," Peggy was saying. "She was all right there. Then we had dinner."

"And what, Peggy?" Parker was having trouble hiding his own impatience. He intended to find out what, or more likely who, was responsible for this travesty. His fist clenched. He had a strong desire to beat the hell out of someone. Anyone!

"Sid and Davey and their girls came by our table and we went to the bar with them for a few minutes," Billy Joe interrupted. "You remember them, Parker. They were on my security team when we went on tour."

"You left Christiana alone in the dining room?" Parker swung around to face him.

"She wanted to be alone, Parker," Peggy said. "She was sad, melancholy, about selling the house, and wanted to be with her thoughts. That's why, later, when she refused to talk to Damon on the phone, I didn't think too much about it. But now . . ." she looked at Parker, confusion wrinkling her forehead. "I just don't know. Something must have happened in that short time we were away from her."

"I know damn well something happened," Parker

said, springing to his feet to pace again. "And I intend to find out what!"

All that work! All that time! All down the drain! And she was making such good progress, too! If his suspicions were correct and Damon Law was at the bottom of this regression of Christiana's, then . . . His fist clenched again. He would take great pleasure in spoiling his pretty face.

"Come on, Peggy. You didn't say anything about this to me." Billy Joe jumped up to join Parker in his pacing.

"No. I thought she had the right to say good-bye to the life she had lived there with Johnny. But now, looking back, something wasn't right when I went back into the dining room. There was a feeling."

"Aw! You women and your feelings," Billy Joe scoffed.

"Now wait a minute, Billy Joe," Parker said. "Don't discount feminine intuition. What do you think happened, Peggy?"

"I have thought about it till my head hurts! Only two things could have happened, Parker. Either someone spoke directly to her, or she overhead something. Whatever, it was enough for her to refuse Damon's call that evening. But . . ." she continued, lifting her hands, "at the airport the next day she greeted him as usual, and couldn't wait to be alone with him." Peggy shook her head. "I just don't *know*. Something happened. Something *muy maldo*."

"Oh, Lord!" Billy Joe muttered. "As if we don't have enough problems, she's startin' to talk foreign!"

"Obviously," Parker said, ignoring Billy Joe's muttered imprecation, "the next step is to talk to Damon Law. Again."

"Again?" Billy Joe's head came up alertly. "What do you mean 'again?'"

"Never mind," Parker said absently. "Do you know where I can find him?"

"Do you think Damon's at the bottom of this?" Billy Joe surged to his feet, ready to do battle. "If he is, I'll beat the living hell out of him."

"You'll have to stand in line. I get him first," Parker growled menacingly.

The moon was sinking in the west when Damon let himself into his lodge at The Woodlands Inn. Mechanically he removed his jacket and tossed it in the direction of the couch. Stepping into the kitchen, he opened the refrigerator and took out a beer. Rummaging in the drawer by the sink for an opener, he jabbed his finger on the tip of a paring knife. Swearing, he sucked on the wounded digit. The tip of his finger in his mouth brought bittersweet memories of the times he had sucked and nibbled on Christiana's fingertips. With a violent oath, he yanked the drawer, spilling the contents onto the floor. Finding the elusive opener, he snapped the top off his beer. The faint hissing sound it made was loud in the empty apartment.

"Got another one of those?"

Damon whirled around, snapping on the light in the living area as he turned. He wasn't surprised to see the man who sat on the couch, his feet propped on the coffee table.

"Hello, Parker," he drawled slowly. "I wondered when you'd show up. I'd ask how you got in, but I'm not sure I want to know." He opened another beer. Looking in the freezer, he took out a frosted stein and turned it up over the long neck. Sauntering into the living room, he handed the beer to Parker, then made himself comfortable in the easy chair.

"Never let it be said I disappoint my friends," Parker said as he poured the cold beer into the stein, being careful not to let the foam run over. "You know why I'm here, of course."

Silently, Damon saluted him with his bottle.

"I'm disappointed in you, Damon. I thought we had a gentleman's agreement."

"Some you win, some you lose," Damon said flippantly.

"You definitely lost this one, my friend. In a big way." Parker drank half his beer in one breath. Putting the glass on the coffee table, he leaned forward. Barely leashed anger radiated from him so powerfully that Damon could feel it all the way across the small room.

"Hell, Damon. I'm not here to rail at you for ending your affair with Christiana. Even though, in my estimation, you're making a big mistake. They broke the mold when they made that woman. However . . ." he leaned back, "that's neither here nor there. What I do object to, and rather violently I'm afraid, is the way you just dropped her, cold."

Damon finished off his beer and made his way carefully into the kitchen. "Want another?" he asked over his shoulder.

"Why not?" Parker answered.

They drank their second beer in silence. Damon, getting up for a third, looked questioningly at Parker. Parker just nodded his head affirmatively. This time he ignored the stein and drank straight from the bottle.

"How about running that by me one more time?" Damon asked, about mid-way through the third beer.

"Run what by you one more time?"

"That part about me dropping Christiana."

"Why? Didn't you understand it the first time around?"

"Can't say that I did, since I'm the droppee rather than the dropper." Damon frowned. "That's not right. Not good English, but you unnerstand what I mean."

"Don't screw around with me," Parker said angrily. "Are you trying to tell me that you didn't drop Christiana?"

"Not tryin' to. *Tellin'* you. Christi was the dropper this time. Got a dose o' my own medicine."

"Damon . . ." Parker leaned forward and looked closely at his friend. "Exactly how many beers have you had tonight?"

"Jus' these . . ."

Parker relaxed. After all, three beers never hurt anyone. He'd seen Damon put away twice that much and never show it.

". . . here. 'Course, that doesn't count the Scotch I had at the country club."

"Oh, hell!" Parker stood up and stomped into the kitchen. Opening the refrigerator, he removed the remaining beer and put it in the empty trash can. Holding the plastic container under one arm, he pocketed the keys to Damon's Vette.

"Damn it, Damon. I can't punch out a drunk, no matter now badly I want to. I'm taking your beer and your car keys. Sober up, and call me tomorrow. We've got some serious talking to do. *Ciao*."

TWELVE

". . . and that's all I know." Damon finished his story and sat back in his chair.

It was early the next afternoon and Damon and Parker were in Parker's study in the house on Lake Conroe.

The well-equipped room was a surprise in a private residence. Parker did not own an ordinary personal computer. He had a high-tech outfit that looked like it should be in the Pentagon. His radio was an elaborate setup that any ham operator would envy. Even more surprising, though, was the way Parker seemed to change when he entered the room. The indolent playboy was gone, and in his place was a hard, sharp-eyed stranger. Damon, surprised by the subtle metamorphosis, found himself changing his opinion of Parker Lloyd.

Parker was leaning back in his large leather chair, his hands linked behind his head. His feet were propped on the top of his executive-sized desk. When Damon finished talking, he stared thoughtfully at him for a minute longer. Then, slapping his hands on the arms of his chair, he sat forward and leaned his elbows on the desktop.

"That's the truth?" he demanded shortly.

"So help me," Damon said, his eyes narrowing on his host. If he weren't so wrapped up in his own troubles, he would like to get to know this new Parker. He would be an interesting friend—and a deadly enemy.

"Umm," Parker murmured. "The more I hear, the more inclined I am to agree with Peggy. Someone spoke to her or she overheard something in the dining room that last night in L.A. But what? Who?"

"I think I know the answers," Damon said. "Just theory and speculation, you understand, but it's the only thing I can come up with that makes sense." He took a deep breath. "I think," he said, exhaling the air in his lungs with a whoosh, "as far out as it sounds, I think Lissa Andrews bought Christi's house as a ruse to get her to L.A. Once she was there, I believe Lissa arranged to 'accidentally' feed Christi a bunch of half-baked truths liberally laced with out-and-out lies."

"Does the Andrews woman hate you that much?" Parker demanded.

"Yes."

"You make strong enemies, my friend," Parker said.

"She also arranged that scene at the airport in Atlanta," Damon continued. "I should have paid more attention to that little episode." Damon went on to tell Parker the two questions Christi had asked him on her return from Los Angeles and the conclusions he had drawn.

"I believe you, Damon. But I can see how it would look, especially to Christiana. She's not the most secure person in the world about relationships since Johnny died. I'm talking about any type of relationship, not just man/woman involvement."

"If I could only get her to listen to me!" Damon said, seething with helplessness. "Explaining the film is no problem. It was in the can before I met Christiana." Damon jumped up and paced the room a couple of times before settling down in his chair again. "But that picture in the paper . . .! What woman wouldn't be hurt by something like that?" He stood up abruptly, looked wildly around the room, then sank into his chair.

"I swear, I didn't know Lissa Andrews was within a thousand miles of Atlanta, but how will I ever prove it? I was just standing there, waiting for my luggage, when suddenly, there she was, clinging to me like a limpet. Hell, Parker. What was it that Paul Newman said? 'Why should I go out for hamburger when I've got steak at home?' My sentiments exactly."

"You relieve my mind. I didn't think I'd made that big a mistake about you. Nice to know I'm not slipping." Parker pushed a button on his elaborately complex desk. "Ready for something cool to drink?"

Damon shuddered.

"Cold orange juice sound okay?" Parker asked understandingly. He spoke quietly into the phone.

"Fine," Damon said absently. He wasn't really interested in anything to drink. "Tell me, Parker. You've known Christiana longer than I. When is she going to calm down enough for me to talk to her?"

"Never."

"You're kidding, I hope," Damon said, startled by the blunt answer.

"Unfortunately, I'm not. For all her good qualities, Christiana, like the rest of us mortals, has some faults.

Not many, mind you. But the ones she has are doozies. Believe me, she has stubbornness honed to a fine art."

"Then I'm shot down." Damon was looking more and more morose as Parker talked.

"Not necessarily," Parker said, a gleam appearing in his eye. "I've dealt with Christiana's stubbornness before. If, just *if* I find a way to make Christiana talk with you, what are your intentions?"

"I'm going to bind her to me in every way I can, legally, morally, and emotionally! Hell, I'll use a damn *rope* if I have to!"

"Good enough. Let me see what I can do and I'll get back to you."

The door opened and his houseboy came in, bearing a tray with a pitcher of fresh-squeezed orange juice and two chilled glasses. He set the tray on Parker's desk and left quietly.

"Cheer up, Damon," Parker said, grinning from ear to ear. "Someone else said, 'The game's not over till the fat lady sings.'" He poured a tall glass of juice and handed it to his unhappy guest. "I don't even hear the orchestra warming up, much less the screeching of a soprano." He laughed at Damon's grimace. "I must tell you, though, I'm getting a kick out of this."

"I always knew you had a sadistic streak a yard wide," Damon groused.

"Hey. Don't be a spoilsport! Not many people get to be in on the fall of a notorious womanizer. I intend to make the most of the opportunity. I'm going to enjoy every second of the next few days." Parker laughed again as Damon pulled a face. "Don't worry, my friend. I won't let you suffer long. Your downfall is going to be swift, and permanent."

* * *

Parker, Peggy, and Billy Joe were in conference in the family room of Christiana's house. Due to some astute managing by Parker, Christiana's parents' had come down from East Texas and taken her out for the day.

"I don't like it." Billy Joe made a chopping motion with his hand.

"I do. I love it. It's very romantic, and it's the only way I know that will get Christi to sit still long enough to listen to Damon," Peggy said, smiling for the first time in days.

"Aw, Peggy, you always did have a soft spot for that guy," Billy Joe protested.

"Yeah. I like him. But, more important than that, Christi loves him."

"You're very sure of this, aren't you, Peggy?" Parker said.

"Yep. It's as obvious as the nose on your face. But some people around here," she stared hard at Billy Joe, "can't see the trees for the forest."

"But, dammit, Parker! To trick her like that! I still don't like it." Billy Joe was going down for the count, but he was going down fighting.

"Can you think of anything else to resolve this impasse?" Parker said coldly.

Billy Joe was silent.

"Okay, then. We go as planned."

Two days later, Billy Joe opened the trunk of the car for the third time and checked to make sure Christiana's case was there. For the third time he saw the light tan case with the brown leather corners. It was still sitting right where he had put it. Slamming the trunk closed, he backed the car into the driveway. Impatiently, nervousness making him belligerent, he stomped into the front hall and stopped at the foot of the stairs. "Christiana!" he yelled. "Hurry up. We'll be late!"

Peggy was putting the finishing touches on Christiana's braids, pinning them in the familiar coronet. "That Billy Joe. Betcha he'll be yelling 'hurry up' to Saint Peter," she laughed softly.

Christiana smiled. A faint smile, but a smile nevertheless. "He was born impatient, Peggy." A wave of sadness swamped her. Damon had always called her "Miss Impatience." She flinched, then bit her lip, holding back the flood of memories. She was on her way to the doctor for her regular eye exam. It would not do for her to show up with red, swollen eyes.

"Yeah," Peggy agreed. "Sometimes Billy Joe would try a saint, but . . ." Biting back the comment that he had reason to be nervous, she pushed the last pin into place. "That'll do, I think. You look very nice, Chris."

"Thanks, Peggy. If I do, it's all due to your efforts." Christiana turned to face her friend. "Have I ever told you how much I appreciate you?"

"So many times I'm gettin' bored hearing it. Now get out of here before Billy Joe has a spasm."

Christiana hugged Peggy and left the room. She was wearing a light wool suit of green heather, with a fitted jacket and dirndl skirt. Her brown calfskin pumps and shoulder bag picked up the dark-brown flecks woven in the material of her suit.

"It's about time." Billy Joe pushed away from the wall and opened the door for her. "It's a nice day for a drive," he said nervously, "even if we are only going into Houston."

"Yes." Christiana did not notice anything out of the ordinary about his behavior. Billy Joe was always a little on the hyper side. "That norther that came through yesterday must have cleared out the cloud cover. I can feel the sun on my face," she said. "It's nice to have a day without rain and drizzle for a change."

"Yeah," Billy Joe said, looking up at the sky instead of at the woman he was helping to set up. "It chased the clouds and smog right out to sea." He backed out into the street and turned toward the Interstate. "But it'll be raining again in a day or so."

"That's for sure," Christiana replied absently. "One thing about Texas. If you don't like the weather, just wait a little while. It'll change."

"Want some music?" Billy Joe asked as they traveled south.

"Yes, please." Christiana was thankful for the music. It filled the interior of the car, and she did not have to strain to make small talk with her friend.

She knew he was worried about her. They all were. Whispered conversations would suddenly cease when she came into a room. And when she was near them, she could sense their concern reaching out to her.

She knew her friends wanted to help her, but there was nothing they could do. There was nothing anyone could do. She had to work through this herself.

They probably thought she was going to go into a deep depression like she did after the accident. It was true she had let the falling-out with Damon throw her the first few days, but she had regained her equilibrium and was coping nicely.

What difference did it make if she cried herself to sleep at night? So what if she jumped when the phone rang or there was a knock at the door? Damon was gone. She had sent him away.

She had done a lot of thinking while lying in her hammock these last two weeks. Damon Law had entered her life—and he had left. It hurt to think about him. She supposed, with a weary sort of acceptance, that it always would. But he had not left her untouched.

Because of him she had been able to do so many things. Things like getting out and going places with confidence. She would no longer cower in her house, afraid of the outside world. She could go anywhere, do anything—well, almost anything—now.

She still needed someone with her, to guide her, but perhaps she would get a guide dog. Dr. Ainsley was always telling her that blind people who had dogs were independent. It was scary to think about depending on a dumb animal, but it would be wonderful to move about without having to lean on her friends. Yes, she had decided, she would definitely think seriously about a dog.

Another thing Damon's presence in her life had brought about was her decision to sell the house in L.A., the house that held so many poignant memories. If Damon had not forced his way into her life, she would still pathetically be holding on to the house and consequently bogged down in her memories of the past.

But, she realized in a moment of revelation, selling the house had not been the central issue. What was really important was that she could think about Johnny now without doubling over in pain. She could remember the love, the laughter, the sharing—all the good things—without feeling lost and guilty because he was gone and she was left behind.

She had lost Damon the way she had always known she would. But she would have what he had given her forever. Freedom. Freedom from guilt because she still lived.

Now, she thought, with a mental clarity she had not felt in many months, *now I can leave the past and get on with living my life!*

"Well, Christiana. We need to talk." Dr. Ainsley took her arm and led her out of the examining room. "We'll go to my office where we can be comfortable."

Christiana prepared herself to listen to his usual spiel. It was the one thing she really hated about these quarterly examinations. It was depressing to go through the inevitable let down that followed a visit to her eye specialist.

In the last week she had taken herself severely in hand. There were several loose ends in her life that needed tightening. One of them was her sight. She had decided to face the fact that she was blind, and she would probably always be blind. She intended for this visit today to be her last unless an emergency of some sort occurred.

"Well, Christiana," Dr. Ainsley repeated jovially, "this is what we've been waiting for. Of course, we'll have to do some more tests. You'll have to check into the hospital, umm," he shuffled some papers around on his desk, "six weeks from next Monday. We have a better than ninety percent chance of success. I'm sure you can live with those odds." He beamed at her like a fond grandparent.

"The hospital?" Christiana said, puzzled. "Why should I have to go there? Is something wrong?"

"Haven't you heard a word I've said?" Dr. Ainsley said, exasperated. "There's nothing wrong. Indeed, no. Everything's right for a change. I believe we're going for that operation, that's all. Of course, it all depends on the outcome of the test we'll do in the hospital, but, as of right now, I don't anticipate any problems."

"Operation?" Christiana said, stunned. "Are you saying that *now* I'll be able to see again?" She listened as Dr. Ainsley repeated his news.

She didn't believe this! An operation! Ninety percent chance of success. Ninety percent virtually meant she was guaranteed her sight would be restored. She'd see again! Now, when nothing mattered anymore. She began to giggle, then laugh. Then she was laughing and crying, and Dr. Ainsley was calling for his nurse.

Half an hour later a still stunned Christiana was led out to the waiting room by the nurse and turned over to Billy Joe's solicitous care.

If she was subdued and a little pale, Billy Joe didn't notice. He had enough troubles of his own.

With lagging steps he led her to the elevator that would take them to the parking garage. He was going to go through with this, but he still didn't like it. Peggy and Parker had both overridden his objections. Naturally, they thought it was a good idea. They liked that s.o.b., Damon Law. Billy Joe still thought he ought to rearrange his face.

In the parking garage, Billy Joe opened the car and helped Christiana into the vehicle. Depressing the locking mechanism on the door, he closed it firmly. Then he walked two cars down and opened the door to Parker's car. Getting in, he glowered at Parker, sitting, calm and unruffled, in the driver's seat. "I still don't like it," he grumbled.

"You worry too much," Parker answered him. "It'll be all right. Just wait and see."

"I hope so," Billy Joe said. "I purely hope so. I'd hate like hell to have to punch you out, too."

Christiana's head was still spinning. An operation! Now! There was no doubt about it. Fate was cruel. She slid down in her seat as the car made the long, sloping drive down to the street level. How many times, she wondered, leaning her body with the sway of the car, had she thought she would give anything if only she could once, just once, look into Damon's eyes? It would have meant so much to her to see his face. If only once she could have seen him smiling at her—to have seen the expression in his eyes, on his face, when they made love.

Damn it, she was doing it again. Just thinking about Damon brought back too many memories. Memories of his voice, his large, strong body, his distinctive scent. She inhaled deeply. She would never forget that scent. His cologne, combined with his own, particular male musk, would always be with her. It was strange, but she thought she could actually smell it now.

She sniffed, then sniffed again, disbelieving her own senses. She wasn't imagining things! There was no doubt about it! Damon was in the car with her! What was worse, he was driving!

"Damon Law, you stop this car right now!"

He laughed. "I wondered when you'd snap, Christi."

"I mean it, Damon. Let me out, right now."

"In the middle of Highway 288? Don't be ridiculous, Christiana."

"What are we doing on 288? This isn't the way back to The Woodlands! Where are you taking me?"

"Why, to Surf Side, of course," he answered cheerfully.

"The hell you are! I want out, and I want out right now! I don't give a damn where we are!" she said, fumbling with the door lock. Then she froze, as a new thought struck her. "How come you're driving my car?"

"How do you think?"

"Billy Joe! He did this? I don't believe it!"

"Believe it, Christiana."

"Noo," she moaned. Betrayed! She had been betrayed by someone she trusted. Her friend. How could Billy Joe do this to her?

She thought he knew how she felt! She thought he understood! If she could not bear to have Damon in her home, with her friends to provide a protective buffer, if it hurt so much she could not even talk to him on the phone, what did Billy Joe think being in the same car with him would do to her?

She was going to fly apart in a million little pieces! No she wasn't! Holding her throbbing temples with her fingertips, she fought to control her ragged emotions. She was here, and there was nothing left for her to do but give in gracefully. For now.

Damon watched Christiana carefully. Like the first time she rode with him, she was again an unwilling passenger. She had settled down and was sitting quietly, with her hands folded in her lap.

He had to force his eyes back to the road. She was so beautiful to him, and it had been so long since he had held her in his arms. He could hardly wait to get her to Surf Side. Already he could feel her hair, sliding through his fingers as he took it down.

Whoa, boy. He put a break on his mental images. *First things first. First, you've got to get her to listen to you. Let you explain.*

They were on the new expressway, speeding toward Angleton and the gulf. There would be no casual drive along the coast this time. He wanted to get Christiana to Surf Side as quickly as possible. Somehow he knew there would be no talking to her until they were closed in the house where they had been so happy together.

If then.

Parker had stressed how stubborn Christiana could be. What if she didn't listen? Damon slammed a lid on his frantic thoughts. She would listen. She had to listen. He would *make* her listen.

Deliberately, he turned his eyes back to the road. Only an hour and a half more, and they would be there. He had come down yesterday and opened up the house. There would be no taking Christiana into a cold, closed up house this time. No way. Today she would enter a warm house. A welcoming house. A house that stood waiting for her.

Christiana stared sightlessly out the car window. How did she get into these situations anyway?

She sighed. Betrayed. By the very person she thought she could trust the most. She still couldn't believe it. *But, that's what you get, Christiana, when you refuse to take your friends into your confidence*, she thought sadly.

But, how could I? she cried silently. *How could I have told them of the humiliation? The betrayal?*

On, damn. If only Damon had told her "no" when she asked her questions. "No," his picture was not about a blind woman. "No," he did not know anything about Lissa Andrews and that awful newspaper picture.

The trip was over all too soon. Too soon, they were at the coast. Too soon, they drove over the high bridge, tall enough for a tanker to pass under, that led from

Freeport to Surf Side. Too soon, they crunched onto the oyster-shell driveway at Damon's beach house.

Damon turned the headlights off. For a moment he just sat, gathering his wits for the coming struggle. So much was riding on the next few hours, he thought. Like the rest of his life! Taking a deep breath he opened his door and got out, stretching his arms above his head.

He was worn out. It had been a long, tense drive. Hell, the last week had been an eternity! He didn't need any added tension. But the strain of waiting for Christiana to come out of her doctor's office had taken its toll on his already taut nerves. There had always been the possibility that they would not get away with what they had planned. She could have realized that it was Damon in the driver's seat and refused to get in the car.

Slowly, he walked around to open Christiana's door. "We're here," he said with forced cheerfulness as he helped her out.

"I know," she said. "I'm not without understanding."

"I came down and opened up yesterday," he told her, ignoring her belligerence. "I wanted it to be nice for you."

"Oh? You were that sure I would be here? Never mind. Don't answer that question. With Billy Joe going behind my back, I suppose you were."

"All I want is a chance to talk to you, Christiana."

Christiana tossed her head and turned away. Suppressing a sigh, Damon took her arm and led her into the house. It was going to be a long night.

Christiana sat stiffly on the couch in front of the free-standing fireplace. She could hear Damon whistling under his breath as he moved around, building up the fire. His cheerfulness only added to her anger, and she was already so damn mad she was about to explode.

Damn Billy Joe! Damn him! What made him think he could get away with this? The nerve of him, turning her over to Damon like that! *Wait until I get hold of you, Billy Joe Chambers,* she thought, tapping her toe angrily on the floor. *Friend or not, I'll fire you so fast you won't know what hit you!*

"There. That's burning nicely," Damon said, standing and brushing off his hands.

So am I, Christiana thought peevishly.

"Are you hungry, Christi?" Damon asked pleasantly, moving toward the kitchen.

Christiana frowned sullenly in his direction. Yes, she was hungry, but she'd be double damned before she would eat with him. She had to keep a tight hold on her rigid anger. If she gave in, even a little, she would throw herself in Damon's arms and beg him to love her.

"Still sulking, Christi?" Damon asked, his voice muffled as he bent over to rummage in the cabinet for a pot. Finding the one he wanted, he straightened up and put it on the stove with a clatter. He took a two quart container of homemade soup from the refrigerator. "I'll have some soup heated up for us soon. Do you want crackers or toast with yours?"

Christiana remained stubbornly silent.

"Warm toast, I think, on such a cold night," Damon said. He continued talking about everyday things as he put the simple meal together.

Christiana folded her arms about her, huddling into the corner of the couch. This was awful! She couldn't stay here. She would *not* stay here! Her mind darted about furiously, trying to find a way out of her predicament. She had to get to the phone to call— Who? Not Billy Joe. That ratfink had betrayed her. Parker! She breathed a sigh of relief. She could call Parker. He was a better choice anyway, because he was sure to know the exact location of Damon's beach house.

Having made up her mind, Christiana relaxed. She could wait. Damon would have to go upstairs sooner or later. When he did, she would call Parker. He would come for her. "Soup's ready, Christiana." She jumped as Damon's voice came from directly over her. She had been so deep in her plans she had not heard him approach.

Frowning sullenly in his direction, she tucked her feet up under her and turned her head away.

Damon sighed. Christiana wasn't going to let this be easy. She was determined to be as difficult and cause him as much trouble as she could. Oh, well. Might as well be hung for a sheep as for a lamb. He bent down and picked her up.

"What are you doing?" she demanded, surprised. "Put me down this instant!"

"Okay, Christi. Whatever you say," Damon said calmly, setting her in a chair at the table. "There you are. Eat hearty. We have soup, toast, and hot tea. The tea's at two o'clock, and toast is ten. The soup and the tea are hot. Be careful, Christi, and don't scald your tongue."

Christiana folded her hands in her lap and prepared to suffer some agonizing minutes. She was hungry, and the soup smelled so good! But she would be damned if she would let him soothe away the fine edge of her anger.

It would be so easy to fall under the spell Damon was weaving about her. So easy to fall for the assumption that everything was as it had been. So easy to believe that nothing had happened to mar their happiness, no angry words spoken, no doors slammed. So easy to believe that he had never used her disability for research, never betrayed her with Lissa Andrews in Atlanta. So easy because she wanted to believe. Listening to the scrape of his spoon against the china soup bowl, she hardened her heart. If she broke down, if she ate, or even talked to Damon, she would be lost.

In spite of the high-handed way he had treated her— he had after all, kidnapped her and brought her here against her will—in spite of his callousness in using her for research, in spite of everything, she still loved him.

Unconsciously, Christiana sighed. It was true. She loved him, and it was pure torture to sit across the table from him like this. She was aware of every move he made.

His hauntingly familiar scent wafted over her as he walked past her to the stove. His cologne was distinctive. If she lived to be a hundred she would never forget it. There was his slightly musky, familiar male scent. And she caught a whiff of tobacco. Had he started smoking again? Because of their fight? A wave of guilt washed over her. But she only felt guilty for a moment. Damon was a grown man, and as such, responsible for his own actions. Though she felt badly about it, she certainly hadn't forced him to resume smoking.

Damon stifled a sigh of resignation. Christiana was still sitting stiffly in her chair, her arms folded across her breasts. He had expected a fight. Parker was right. She was sure as hell the most stubborn woman he had ever come across.

"Loosen up, Christi." His chair scraped the floor as

he pulled it out and sat down. "You're just making it hard on yourself. You're here, and here you'll stay until I'm ready to let you go. So you might as well eat your supper."

"Drop dead!"

THIRTEEN

"Ah," he taunted, laughing, "she has a tongue after all."

Christiana, furious with herself for letting him goad her into speech, clamped down hard on her traitorous tongue.

Damon, reading her face as easily as he always had, laughed again. She was stubborn, all right, but he was even more stubborn. He had no doubt about who would ultimately win this duel of wills. He just had to be patient.

He finished his supper and began clearing his end of the table. "Still haven't eaten, Christi? Perhaps you like cold soup?" He turned the water on in the sink.

Damon finished washing his few dishes. Drying his hands, he leaned down and placed his arms on the table, pinning Christi in. "Eat, Christiana. I'll not have you getting sick because of your foolishness."

Christiana bit her tongue so hard she could taste

blood. She would not give him the satisfaction of letting him prod her into speaking again.

She could hear Damon moving around the living room area. He added more wood to the fire and replaced the screen. Then he walked over to the door and rattled the latch, making sure it was secure for the night. The creaking of the couch springs, along with his sigh, told her he was making himself comfortable. A moment later, she heard the sound of magazine pages being turned.

Knowing that Damon was sitting on the soft couch irritated her. Her bottom was already getting numb from the lengthy contact with the hard wood of the kitchen chair. Chalking up one more grievance, she prepared herself for a long wait. Sooner or later he had to go upstairs. Then it would be just a matter of reaching over, picking up the telephone, and calling Parker. She could wait, she thought, trying to get some feeling in her benumbed bottom by wiggling about on the chair. She could wait all night if she had to.

After a while she heard Damon stirring around. His footsteps came toward the table. She felt his eyes on her. Resolutely, she turned her head away from him. He was willing her to weaken. She could literally feel him demanding that she give in. He stood over her for a minute or two, causing her extreme discomfort, before he went up the stairs. When she heard his steps overhead, she reached for the phone.

The soft burring sound of the distantly ringing phone sounded in her hear. "Come on, Parker," she whispered. "Answer the damn phone."

Overhead, Damon's footsteps moved toward the stairs. Panic-stricken, Christiana jerked her head up to listen. The steps turned back toward the bathroom and she breathed a sigh of relief.

She was about to despair of anyone answering at Parker's when she heard Parker's houseboy say, "Lloyd residence."

"Miguel? Put Parker on, quick!" she whispered.

"Señora Smith? That is you?"

"Yes, it's me. Get Parker for me. Now!"

"*Sí, señora. Pronto.*"

"Christiana? Hi, honey, how's it going?" Parker's voice was a welcome sound in a world turned upside down.

"Parker! Do you know where Damon's beach house is?"

"Is that where you are? Did you and Damon get everything straightened out? Has Damon convinced you that he loves you yet?"

"Did we *what*? Parker Lloyd!" she wailed, "were you in on this, too?" She forgot to whisper as she demanded an answer. Her suspicions were growing stronger by the minute.

"In on it? Hell, Christi, it was my idea!"

Parker, too! First Billy Joe, then Parker—or was it the other way around?

She was so shocked she barely realized when Damon took the receiver from her numb fingers. "Parker? Yeah, she is . . . uh huh . . . yeah, I'll do that," he laughed. "So long."

Damon replaced the phone, then stood over Christiana, jingling the change in his pocket. "I guess you can tell I'm new at this kidnapping business," he said finally. "I didn't think about the phone." He looked at her untouched food. "I'll warm that up for you. You have to eat, Christi."

Stunned by the knowledge that Parker had planned this fiasco, Christiana mechanically picked up her spoon and began to eat the reheated soup. It was while she was scooping up the last of the soup that the rest of what Parker said registered. *Has Damon convinced you that he loves you yet?*

Parker was saying that Damon loved her!

Damon watched her for a minute or so, then walked back into the living area to sink wearily down in front of the fire. This was going to take longer than he had planned.

Damn it, she was breaking his heart! She was hurt by what she considered her friends' betrayal. And stubborn! God! Was she stubborn! He wasn't as sure of himself now as he had been before he brought her here.

He looked up to see Christiana standing in front of him. "Where do I sleep?" she asked, snapping the words out.

"Upstairs, of course."

"Thank you," she said stiffly. "I'll turn in now, if you don't mind."

"Sure. Go ahead." Damon watched her disappear up the stairs. It was all he could do to restrain himself from lifting her in his arms and carrying her to bed. But the proud tilt of her head, coupled with her cool, touch-me-not attitude, held him back.

He had put a big dent in her pride, not only by bringing her here against her will but by going behind her back and using her friends. He had to give her time. Time to adjust to the supposed betrayal of her friends, and time to realize that, sooner or later, she would have to listen to him.

He followed her upstairs. The bathroom door was

firmly shut. He had no doubt that it was locked as well. "Christiana?"

"What?"

"Your case is on the vanity."

"My case?"

"Yeah. Peggy packed you some things."

"Peggy, too?" she said mournfully.

"Yes, dammit! Peggy, too! She loves you. So do Billy Joe and Parker. All they want is for you to be happy!"

"They love me, too?" she said incredulously, her voice rising to a screech. *"Too?"*

"Yes!"

Her head was spinning! Parker had implied that Damon brought her here because he loved her. Damon had said that Parker, Peggy, and Billy Joe loved her, *too*. Was he telling her that he loved her? Then why, in heaven's name, didn't he just say so? He knew she wasn't good at deciphering innuendos! She had to have it spelled out, in black and white!

Christiana belted her robe snugly around her waist and opened the bathroom door. She had dawdled as long as she could, creaming her face, her arms, her legs. Then she had brushed her waist-length hair until it felt like satin under her fingertips, and twisted it in one fat braid that hung over her shoulder. She wasn't sure what would greet her when she left the fragile safety of the bathroom. Finally, unable to put it off any longer, she opened the door.

She faced the bed, then stopped. She was not ready to crawl into that bed, the bed where she and Damon had lain, all tangled in the sheets after making love. She would never be ready.

But she was exhausted. It had been a long, tiring

day. Her brain was spinning trying to figure out if Damon really loved her or if it was all wishful thinking on her part. And, in all practicality, she had to sleep somewhere.

Listening intently, she tried to place Damon's whereabouts in the house. She knew he was inside, she could feel his presence. . . . But where?

When she couldn't hear him, she decided that he must already be asleep on the couch in front of the fire. She left the bathroom door and walked toward the bed with confident steps.

The creaking of the bedsprings halted her in her tracks. They creaked again as a heavy weight shifted on the mattress. Then she heard a soft thunk as a shoe hit the floor. Now she knew where Damon was, and it wasn't on the couch downstairs!

"What do you think you are doing?" she asked icily.

"Getting ready for bed," he said matter-of-factly. The other shoe hit the floor and the mattress creaked again as Damon stood. She heard the unmistakable rustle of his shirt being pulled out of his pants. Then came the faint rasping sound of a zipper. He was undressing!

Grasping the rail, Christi made her way to the stairs. There was no way she was going to sleep in that bed with Damon Law.

"Where do you think you're going?" Damon said sharply.

"Downstairs, to sleep on the couch."

"Oh, no, you're not!" With a bound, Damon was ahead of her, blocking her way. "You're going to sleep in that bed—with me."

"On a cold day in hell!" she spat, trying to move around him. As much as she loved him, if she got in that bed she would be lost. She was strongly tempted to give in. If she did, she would only be hurt again. And she would never survive a second time.

Damon's temper, stretched almost to the breaking point several times during the last few hours, snapped.

Ducking his shoulder against her stomach, he threw Christi over his shoulder. Caught off guard for a moment, she recovered quickly and began screaming. "Damn you, Damon Law! Put me down! Put me down this instant!" Balling her fists, she beat futilely at his rear, which was the only part of him she could reach.

Carrying her to the bed, Damon dumped her unceremoniously onto the fluffy down comforter. Dropping down beside her, he held her in place by the simple expedient of grasping her wrists in one hand and throwing a leg over her thighs. He was panting, partly from exertion but mostly from sheer, unadulterated anger.

"I've had it with you, Christiana! I am now going to explain, and you are going to listen!"

"No!" Christiana said, struggling to get away from him. "I don't want to hear it!"

"Yes, Christiana. I'm going to tell you all about the film, and about my relationship with Lissa Andrews."

"I don't want to talk about either thing. I just want to forget it," she said stubbornly.

"First, about the film. It is about a blind woman. It was also completed and in the can before I met you.

"As for Lissa . . ." He paused, trying to think of a way to say what he had to without sounding like a hotshot playboy. Deciding that the best thing was to jump in and get it over with, he said, "I had an affair with Lissa Andrews a couple of years ago. She didn't want to accept it when it was over. I finally had to have her removed, forcibly, from my house. It was . . . messy. Lissa became very hysterical.

"When she was finally carried, kicking and screaming, to her car, the last thing I heard her say was that she would make me pay someday. She threatened me again the same afternoon I met you.

"Gossip spreads quickly in the film industry. There were people in Hollywood who knew I was serious about you before I knew it myself. When Lissa heard, she knew she had her instrument of revenge. How she found out I would be at the airport in Atlanta that day, I don't know. But there she was, waiting, with a photographer. Honest to God, Christi," his voice was anguished, "I didn't know she was there until she threw herself at me."

Christiana was silent for a minute, thinking about the vindictive woman she had overheard talking in L.A. The woman she heard was capable of doing something like Damon described. She gasped as another thought struck her. Lissa Andrews was also capable of setting up that scene in the hotel dining room!

Christi had let that woman's hate destroy what she had with Damon. She hadn't trusted him. She didn't deserve Damon or his love. With a loud wail, she turned away from him.

Damon propped himself up on his elbow and stared at her. Christiana was crying. His Christiana, whom he would give his life to protect, was crying, and it was his fault.

Smothering a curse, he swung himself up to a sitting position on the side of the bed, holding his head in his hands.

Damn! What had he done? He dragged his hands roughly down his face, rubbing his mouth and chin with his palms.

He had blown it, that's what he'd done. He, who

was going to be so patient and gentle, had lost his temper. He held his hands tightly over his mouth as he reluctantly recalled the events of the last few minutes.

He remembered Christiana standing at the head of the stairs, defiantly telling him that it would be a cold day in hell. Then, in a real cave-man style, he had thrown her over his shoulder, and tossed her on the bed. *Way to go, Law. You're a real diplomat, you are!*

How long he sat there, heaping coals of fire on his head, Damon did not know. He continued to stare sightlessly ahead. With sharp, agonizing clarity he realized that the long, empty tunnel he had glimpsed weeks ago at Parker's party was nothing compared to the void his life would be from this night on.

Hesitantly, he reached out his hand to Christiana. She looked so small and defenseless, he wanted to take her in his arms and comfort her.

Fool! The last thing she wants is your touch!

"Christiana . . ." He tried to speak, but his voice croaked. Clearing his throat, he tried again. "Get dressed, Christi, and I'll take you home."

Christiana turned onto her back.

"Home?" That was it, then.

Bleakly, Damon watched Christiana swing her legs off the edge of the bed and tighten the belt of her robe. A cold feeling spread in his gut as he faced the fact that his impatience had just killed forever any chance he might have had with her.

"It's funny," he said softly, not realizing he was speaking out loud. "I didn't believe in love, you know. I only set out to seduce you, to see if I could pry you away from your past." He laughed mirthlessly. "I wanted to turn you into a 'merry widow.'" His voice became hard and self-accusing.

Christiana flinched. She had known this all along, of course, but it hurt, oh how it hurt, to hear it from Damon's lips.

"You weren't supposed to work your way into my heart . . . become more important to me than the very air I breathe.

"You sure as hell wouldn't win any beauty contest." His bark of laughter was more of a cough than a laugh. "You're flat-chested," he muttered. He was shaking his head in bewilderment. "How could I fall for a flat-chested woman?"

"I never heard you complaining," she said, stung by his apparent callousness.

"Of course you didn't. Do you know why? You're perfect, that's why. Perfect for me in every way." He dropped his head in his hands and Christiana had to strain to hear what he said next. "I love you, you know." he said nonchalantly.

"No. I didn't know," she said, surprise stopping her in her tracks.

"Well, I do." His voice was slightly belligerent. "For all the good it's going to do me now."

"Damon?" she said wonderingly, moving closer to him.

"I've lost it, haven't I, Christi? I've lost it all. You loved me, and I threw it away."

Christiana couldn't make out what he said next. She thought it sounded like, "Arrogant bastard. Stupid, arrogant son-of-a-bitchin' bastard!", but she couldn't be sure. The words were all tangled up with the wrenching sob that seemed to tear its way from his throat.

Sobs? From Damon? She knelt before him and touched his face with her fingertips. When she felt the tears on his cheeks, she jerked her hand away. Somehow, it seemed an invasion of privacy to be a witness to his grief.

And why did he grieve? Because of her. Because he thought he had lost her love. Love! Damon loved her! Christiana could barely breathe as the wonder of it hit her.

"I-love-you-Damon-Law." The words came tumbling out, running together in her haste to let him know his love was returned. "I love you," she said again, slowly and deliberately.

Damon lifted his bowed head to stare at her. "What? What did you say?" he asked, doubting his own senses.

"I said, 'I love you, Damon Law.'"

"You do?" Christiana could not see the light of hope that flared in his eyes, but she heard it in his voice.

"Yes. I do and I'm so sorry. Can you ever forgive me for not having more faith in you?"

"If you'll forgive me for being so slow to recognize love when I came face-to-face with it," Damon said, kissing her hungrily. "Christiana. Christi. Love." Damon caressed her face in his hands, holding her like she was a priceless treasure. "Oh, Christi. I love you. I *love* you!"

Pulling her up into his lap, he kissed her. It was a gentle kiss, a reverent kiss, a kiss that said all the things he felt but was unable to put into words.

He buried his face in her neck, holding her tightly to him, afraid that if he let go she would disappear.

They sat that way for a long time, Damon gently rocking to and fro; Christiana holding on for all she was worth.

"Love me, Damon," she said at last.

"Christi?" he asked wonderingly.

"Please? Love me?"

"Christiana!" Damon was amazed. She never ceased to fascinate him, this tall, brown-eyed, *beautiful* woman of his.

"Aren't you going to love me?" she asked plaintively.

"Oh, yes. Yes, Christi, my love!"

Damon tangled his hands in her braid as he bent to kiss her. His lips brushed hers softly, questioningly. Christiana pulled his head down to her, deepening the kiss. With a shout of triumph Damon tightened his arms around her. They fell, laughing onto the bed.

"Say it again, Christiana," Damon said between kisses as he worked his way down her throat to her breasts.

"Say what?" Christiana gasped, hugging him to her with all her strength.

"Tell me you love me," Damon demanded.

"Greedy," Christiana accused.

"Oh, yes! Yes, I'm greedy. I want to hear you say it. I'll never hear it enough!" Damon said wonderingly.

"Then, I'll have to tell you and tell you until you believe me," Christiana said, understanding what he was saying. "And you'll have to tell me."

Propping himself up on his elbows, Damon brushed her hair out of her face. "I love you, Christiana Smith," he said seriously. "I've loved you for a long time, but I didn't have sense enough to know it." He kissed her eyes, her cheek, her lips. "I'll love you for the rest of my life, and beyond. I'll love you forever."

"As I'll love you, my love," Christiana said softly.

Their lovemaking was gentle at first. Each was afraid of pushing the other. Then the passion grew as they began touching each other, remembering. They were each intent on showing the other their love. Touching, kissing, loving, they rode the rising waves, letting their physical joining set the seal on their vows. As they reached the crest, Christiana clung to Damon, knowing he would always be her anchor in a turbulent world. Damon, peaking right along with Christiana, cried, "You're mine, Christi. You're mine!"

"Yes, yours," Christiana sighed as she sank into the cushion of Damon's love.

Christiana woke with a start. Someone was staring at her. She could feel it. That wasn't all she could feel. Under her neck was a strong, rock-hard arm. Across her legs was the heavy weight of a hairy, masculine leg. Against her thigh was . . .

"Damon," she sighed.

"Yes, love?"

"It wasn't a dream." She sighed again as she snuggled against his big body, happy and secure for the first time in weeks.

"Not unless we both dreamed the same dream at the same time," Damon said, delighted with her response.

"I don't think that's possible," she said, frowning thoughtfully.

"Neither do I. So I guess we can be sure it wasn't a dream." Damon shifted and looked down at Christiana, who was still blinking sleepily.

"Oh," Christiana said weakly. "Everything's okay, then?"

"Of course it is," Damon growled arrogantly. "You're not angry at me for kidnapping you?" His free hand ran possessively up and down her neck.

"Not even a little bit. It sure spiced up a routine visit to the doctor."

"By the way, Christi," he said as he ran hot little

kisses down her cheek and over her chin, "I've been meaning to ask you. What did your doctor have to say?"

"What doctor?" Christiana said, bemused by his kiss.

"Your eye doctor, Christi," he prompted.

"Oh! *That* doctor! You'll never believe this! Oh, Damon! Have I got news!"

The orchestra was playing soft, romantic melodies, perfect for slow dancing. The bar at the end of the patio was doing a landslide business in imported champagne. Gardenias and exotic orchids, specially flown in from Hawaii, floated on the surface of the Olympic-size pool, their heady fragrance perfuming the afternoon air.

Damon held his wife's hand as he pushed his way through the crowd. Shrugging his broad shoulders, he broke away from the wedding guests. He'd had enough of the crowd, enough of the back-slapping and congratulations, and more than enough of the sly grin on Parker Lloyd's face. He loosened his tie and unbuttoned his collar as he made his way across the perfectly manicured lawn to the gravel path hidden in the thick trees that surrounded Parker's lakeside estate.

The sky above them was a brilliant blue. The deep blue that only a Texas sky can be after a norther has blown through. The afternoon sun had brought the temperature on this winter day to the midseventies.

The gravel path that wandered through the trees was almost obscured by fallen leaves, but the deck that jutted out over the creek was clean—and empty. That deck, and a few moment's privacy, was their destination.

Christiana laughed breathlessly as they stepped up onto the deck. "Are we where I think we are?"

"That's right, Christiana. Right back where it all started." He pulled her into his arms and kissed her until she was even more breathless.

"I love you, Christiana Law. So very much. But I'll have to admit I'm glad that circus is over. I want to shout to the world that you're mine, and I guess that a wedding is as good a way as any to do it, but I'd have been just as happy standing up in front of the justice of the peace."

"But Parker, Peggy, and Billy Joe all put up such a fuss when we suggested a private ceremony."

"Yeah. They just wanted to gloat. It's a good thing that everything turned out all right. Parker's plan almost backfired into a catastrophe!" Pulling her into his arms, he kissed her thoroughly. "Hello, Mrs. Law."

"Hello, yourself, Mr. Law," she grinned up at him. He took her face in his hands and kissed her possessively. "Christiana? Christi? Are you sure you wanted to marry me? I didn't steamroller you?"

"Yes, I'm sure, and no, you didn't." She snuggled against him, holding him tight.

"There's one thing *I* know for certain," Damon said positively as he placed a kiss on her brow. "This is absolutely the last one of Parker Lloyd's parties *you're* going to attend!"

SHARE THE FUN . . .
SHARE YOUR NEW-FOUND TREASURE!!

You don't want to let your new books out of your sight? That's okay. Your friends can get their own. Order below.

No. 5 A LITTLE INCONVENIENCE by Judy Christenberry
Never one to give up easily, Liz overcomes every obstacle Jason throws in her path and loses her heart in the process.

No. 6 CHANGE OF PACE by Sharon Brondos
Police Chief Sam Cassidy was everyone's protector but could he protect himself from the green-eyed temptress?

No. 7 SILENT ENCHANTMENT by Lacey Dancer
She was elusive and she was beautiful. Was she real? She was Alex's true-to-life fairy-tale princess.

No. 8 STORM WARNING by Kathryn Brocato
The tempest on the outside was mild compared to the raging passion of Valerie and Devon—and there was no warning!

No. 13 SIEGE OF THE HEART by Sheryl McDanel Munson
Nick pursues Court while she wrestles with her heart and mind.

No. 14 TWO FOR ONE by Phyllis Herrmann
What is it about Cal and Elliot that has Leslie seeing double?

No. 15 A MATTER OF TIME by Anne Bullard
Does Josh *really* want Christine or is there something else?

No. 16 FACE TO FACE by Shirley Faye
Christi's definitely not Damon's type. So, what's the attraction?

Kismet Romances
Dept 1090, P. O. Box 41820, Philadelphia, PA 19101-9828

Please send the books I've indicated below. Check or money order only—no cash, stamps or C.O.D.'s (PA residents, add 6% sales tax). I am enclosing $2.75 plus 75¢ handling fee for *each* book ordered.

Total Amount Enclosed: $_____.

___ No. 5   ___ No. 7   ___ No. 13   ___ No. 15
___ No. 6   ___ No. 8   ___ No. 14   ___ No. 16

Please Print:
Name_____
Address_____Apt. No._____
City/State_____ Zip_____

Allow four to six weeks for delivery. Quantities limited.

Kismet Romances has for sale a Mini Handi Light to help you when reading in bed, reading maps in the car, or for emergencies where light is needed. Features an on/off switch; lightweight plastic housing and strong-hold clamp that attaches easily to books, car visor, shirt pocket, etc. 11" long. Requires 2 "AA" batteries (not included). If you would like to order, send $9.95 each to: Mini Handi Light Offer, P.O. Box 41820, Phila., PA 19101-9828. PA residents must add 6% sales tax. Please allow 8 weeks for delivery. Supplies are limited.